"I have to

"And I want *you* to help me find the right woman." Jordan grabbed hold of Elise's hands.

She gasped, unable to believe what he was saying.

"Don't you see?" he continued. "This is perfect. You know all there is to know about romance. With your help, this will work."

Elise was devastated. Here she stood, aroused from the touch of his strong hands and the nearness of his warm body, and he was dead serious. He obviously had no idea how much he affected her, how much she wanted him. She drew away and crossed the room. "Jordan, I really don't think—"

He followed behind her and grasped her shoulders with his hands. "If you help me, and I pull this off by the damn deadline, I'll double your fee as the wedding consultant."

She turned to look at him. Could she do it? Could she bury her feelings of desire for this man and help him find a wife?

Kate Hoffmann has written two fantastic books for Temptation and she's quickly become a dynamic new addition to our exciting lineup of authors. Lucky for us, she entered Temptation's annual contest for unpublished members of the Romance Writers of America in 1992. Her story, *Wanted: Wife,* was so outstanding, she won first place! We asked Kate why she chose to write about a wedding consultant and a man in need of a bride. She explained, ''My sister got married shortly before I began working on this book, and I wanted to write about the crazy atmosphere of organizing a wedding.'' We're sure readers will agree that *Wanted: Wife* is a real winner!

Books by Kate Hoffmann

HARLEQUIN TEMPTATION
456—INDECENT EXPOSURE

WANTED: WIFE
KATE HOFFMANN

Harlequin Books

TORONTO • NEW YORK • LONDON
AMSTERDAM • PARIS • SYDNEY • HAMBURG
STOCKHOLM • ATHENS • TOKYO • MILAN
MADRID • WARSAW • BUDAPEST • AUCKLAND

To my mom and dad,
whose romance is an inspiration to me.
Here's to forty-three years and many more!

ISBN 0-373-25575-6

WANTED: WIFE

Copyright © 1994 by Peggy Hoffmann.

This edition published by arrangement with Harlequin Enterprises B. V.

® and TM are trademarks of the publisher. Trademarks indicated with
® are registered in the United States Patent and Trademark Office, the
Canadian Trade Marks Office and in other countries.

Printed in U.S.A.

1

"YOU COULD always try dating a woman for longer than two months," Pete Stockton commented.

The Sunday edition of the *Chicago Tribune* lay across the wide glass-topped desk, open to the society pages. Jordan Prentiss sat in his leather chair, staring at a photograph of himself and his current companion at a recent charity affair.

When his executive assistant spoke, Jordan looked up in surprise, having forgotten that Pete was still in the room. "I've dated a lot of women for longer than that," he replied.

Pete smiled and shook his head.

"I haven't?" Jordan asked.

"No, I'm afraid not."

"What about Clarise Sheppard?"

"Seven weeks."

Jordan frowned. "It seemed like years," he said absentmindedly as he picked up the paper and scrutinized the brief article beneath the photo:

Jordan Prentiss, bachelor-about-town, with his current lady-in-waiting, Alicia DuMont, attended the recent opening of the new orthopedic wing at Children's Memorial Hospital. Prentiss and his firm, BabyLove Baby Foods, were major contributors to the project.

His gaze drifted back to the photo. After a long pause, he spoke again. "This isn't good, is it?" he murmured. The rhetorical tone of his statement solicited no response from his assistant. When it came to business, Jordan rarely sought or accepted the advice or counsel of others.

Prentiss has the uncanny ability to assess a situation in one second and integrate a fully refined business strategy in the next. Prentiss, a loner by nature, runs his company with absolute authority, maintaining a reserved distance from his management staff. His business tactics are cold and competent, and unquestionably brilliant.

When nosy reporters weren't examining his personal life in the society pages, their counterparts from the business news were carefully dissecting his professional life. He had taken over the helm at BabyLove four years ago, and at the age of thirty-four had become the youngest CEO in the history of the food industry. The business press had hailed him as a wunderkind and watched with interest as he turned a failing, family-owned company around. The following year, the gossip columnists named him one of Chicago's "most eligible." Yet through it all, Jordan thought he had managed to keep his private and his professional life completely separate. Until today.

The bad news had filtered through the office grapevine and ended up on his desk in the form of a ten-page report from Pete. "Are you sure about your information?" Jordan asked, glancing down at the report.

Pete regarded him seriously. "If I wasn't sure, I wouldn't have brought it to you. Your cousin is maneuvering for control of BabyLove and he has some in-fluential board members behind him. He's got until the next board meeting to plead his case. That's just three months away. Edward may not have much business sense, but the guy has a real knack for exploiting a sit-uation. He's convinced the board that as a bachelor, you couldn't possibly represent the wholesome, fam-ily image that BabyLove Baby Foods needs to convey to the public. The media's fascination with your mar-ital status hasn't helped. You've been photographed with six different women in as many months."

Jordan stood and walked to the wall of windows. He gazed down at the bumper-to-bumper Chicago traffic from his vantage point twenty-three stories above Mi-chigan Avenue. "They think Edward would make a better president simply because he's married and has four children." His voice was even and unemotional. "This company was on the edge of bankruptcy when I took over the presidency. Give me another four years and we'll own the baby-food market. I'm the one who's saved this company, not Edward."

"And you've done it by bullying the board into do-ing things your way. They're a conservative bunch, Jordan, and they've never felt comfortable with your progressive ideas about running BabyLove—both you and I know that. You've convinced them to overextend the company and they're scared. Edward would make a much more malleable president."

"Edward would fail inside of a year," Jordan said dryly. "He'd take the company my grandfather founded right along with him. And when Edward failed, the board would be free to appoint someone outside the family. BabyLove has always been run by a Prentiss. I'm not about to let that change."

The office was silent for a long minute before Jordan turned around and took his place behind his desk. He neatly folded the newspaper and dropped it into the wastebasket. "What do you suggest?"

Pete looked taken aback for a moment, then regained his usual composure. "You want my opinion?" the young man asked guardedly.

Jordan nodded. "Of course I do. That *is* what I pay you for, isn't it? Show me some of that Harvard M.B.A. stuff."

Pete sat down across from Jordan, an earnest expression on his face as he spoke. "First, I think you should meet individually with each of the board members, preferably in a neutral setting. Feel them out, find out where they stand. Then lay the facts out on the table and remind them of what you've done for this company. Throw some numbers at them. Play up your close relationship with your grandfather. They loved the old man."

"Is that all?"

Pete shifted uncomfortably in his chair, then handed Jordan a manila envelope. "If that doesn't work, you should consider using these."

Jordan opened the envelope and pulled out a stack of glossy eight-by-tens, each one featuring a buxom young woman, in various stages of undress, and his cousin Edward, in various stages of undressing her. The young woman was not Edward's wife, but by the looks of the photos, she was performing well beyond what was expected of one's marital partner.

Jordan placed the photos back in the envelope and slid them across the desk. "Burn those. Be sure you get the negatives and destroy them, too."

Pete took the photos, his face coloring slightly. "I'm sorry. I just thought—"

"Don't be sorry. You were doing your job. I'm impressed by your instincts about Edward. I never would have suspected."

"But using these photos would put Edward right under your thumb. You could end his interference here and now."

"Edward isn't the problem. The board is." Jordan laughed. "You've got to admire the old man," he added in a cynical voice. "He still controls this company, even from the grave. He chose the board before he died. They're all pillars of the community, happily married, active in their churches, carbon copies of my grandfather, right down to their conservative little business minds. To them, a stable home life equates with a stable business life. It's me they're uncomfortable with. If they couldn't replace me with Edward, they'd find someone else. Some mundane, middle-aged corporate yes-man with a wife, a house in the suburbs, and 2.3 children."

"So what are you going to do?"

"I'm going to woo them individually as you suggest. I'm going to pander to their conservative natures." Jordan paused before he continued, wondering if the decision he had made was too rash. But his company was at stake and he would do anything in his power to save it. "And I'm going to get married."

Jordan was amazed at how easily he said the words. He had never thought marriage was in his future, but when faced with the possibility of losing his company, the decision seemed unavoidable. If possessing a wife would ensure his control of BabyLove, then that's what had to be done. He had no choice in the matter.

The look of shock on Pete's face gradually turned to undisguised admiration. "That's not a bad idea, but the next board meeting is on April 23. They might still vote you out."

"April 18 is a Saturday, isn't it?"

Pete nodded.

"That's the date, then. I want you to start to make plans for the wedding. It has to be very big and very traditional. And I want it kept under wraps until the invitations go out."

Pete held out his hands in a gesture of reluctance. "Wait a second. I don't know anything about planning a wedding."

"Then find someone who does."

Jordan watched his assistant mentally scrambling for an alternative plan. Though he had asked Pete Stockton to do a great many things over the past two years, planning a wedding was the only task well outside his job description. But the young man was hungry and Jordan knew he would find a way of pleasing the boss.

"My sister got married last year," Pete said, his expression brightening, "and she used a wedding consultant."

"Good, get the name of the place and have my secretary make an appointment for you. I think we can trust Sandra to be discreet about our plans. But she's the only other person I want to know about this wedding, outside of you and your wedding person."

"And the bride, of course," Pete added. "Jordan, *she's* supposed to plan the wedding, not her fiancé's business associate. Don't you think Alicia is going to want some say in the matter?"

Jordan looked at him coolly.

"You're not going to marry Alicia?"

Jordan didn't shake his head, merely raised an eyebrow in reply.

"You don't have a bride yet, do you?" Pete groaned in frustration. "Why do I feel like I'm always operating one time zone behind you?"

"I'll take care of finding a bride. You make up the guest list and hire that consultant."

"You're going to have to get involved in the planning. There are all sorts of decisions to be made and it's going to look very suspicious if neither the bride nor the groom is involved. If it leaks out to the press that you're short a fiancée, every unattached female in the city will be pounding down your door. And the board will be right behind them, questioning your motives. Don't you read your own press? Last year you were named Chicago's most eligible bachelor."

"Don't exaggerate the situation. I wasn't the *most* eligible bachelor. I was third on the list."

"That was the year before," Pete said.

Jordan scowled. "All right, I'll go see the wedding consultant, make a few decisions, then let her take over. Have Sandra make an appointment for me this afternoon. In the meantime, I want you to get me a short list of candidates by the end of the day."

"Candidates?"

"Women. Brides-to-be. Preferably over thirty, never married, spotless reputation, well educated."

"I haven't seen any unmarried saints strolling down Michigan Avenue lately," Pete said, a hint of sarcasm in his voice. "But I'll call Rome and have them send five over on the next boat. Anything else?"

Jordan ignored his assistant's remarks. "Yes. They have to be practical. I'm looking for a corporate wife. Someone who understands that this marriage is strictly a business arrangement and nothing more." He picked up a copy of the *Wall Street Journal* and opened it on his desk. "After all, I'm thirty-eight years old," he added distractedly. "It's about time I got married. But I've got a business to run, with precious little time to spend pleasing a wife. So just be sure to avoid incurable romantics with dreams of wedded bliss."

"Five frigid saints. I'll get right on it." Pete walked to the door, but Jordan's next command halted his retreat.

"And Pete, have Sandra send Alicia two dozen roses and my regrets that I won't be able to see her in the near future. You know, pressing business matters . . ."

"Your standard 'Dear Joan' letter?"

He looked up from the newspaper. "Just do it."

Jordan watched the office door close behind Pete, then rose slowly and walked to the windows. His dispassionate gaze traced the path of a bright-yellow cab as it wove its way through the traffic.

Had he made the right choice? Was marriage the only answer? For the first time in his professional life, Jordan found himself questioning one of his business decisions. And the plan to marry *was* purely a business decision. What else could it be? Certainly not personal.

Jordan had never invested much time or effort in his relationships with the opposite sex. Throughout his entire adult life he had found women disturbingly unpredictable and illogical, and frustrating to say the least. Though he tried to maintain a discreet distance from the fair sex, women seemed strangely attracted to him. He couldn't understand why. He gave them no encouragement, no indication of an interest in a long-term relationship, yet he never lacked for female companionship.

Jordan had come to the conclusion that the only thing that kept the women coming back was his money and the power it represented. And the blind hope that they might one day assume the role of Mrs. Jordan Prentiss and thereby capture the keys to the Prentiss family fortune.

If only he had a better understanding of women. Maybe then, the decision to marry wouldn't cause such unaccustomed self-doubt. But his ascent to the presidency of BabyLove had left little time for polishing his social skills. His father had died prematurely of a heart attack when Jordan was sixteen, and from that moment on, his grandfather had begun to groom a shy and rather clumsy teenager to take over the reins of the family business.

Tutors had been hired to accelerate Jordan's prep-school graduation. He completed his college business degree in only three years, studying frantically and working part-time at BabyLove. His M.B.A. had followed two years later, achieved while holding down a junior management position in the marketing department. There had been barely enough time to eat and sleep, certainly no time for school dances and dinner dates.

Over the next twelve years, he had become single-minded in his goal, to the exclusion of anything that remotely resembled a personal life. Jordan had wanted the presidency more than anything. And as a defense against the rampant rumors of nepotism, he had distanced himself from his co-workers. Each business decision had been watched and analyzed by every manager above and below him on the corporate ladder. To avoid the chance of a misstep, he had studied every piece of relevant data before making any business decision, then made the decision with an icy competence that even the most vociferous of his detractors could not fault. After a time, he had gained the respect he deserved. And with it, he had also gained a reputation as a total enigma.

No one knew the real Jordan Prentiss. And at times, he wondered if he even knew himself.

But he did know one thing. He would do anything to save his company. And if that meant getting married, so be it.

THE SUNDAY EDITION of the *Chicago Tribune* lay across Elise Sinclair's desk, open to the society pages. She scanned the engagement listings, scribbling down names as she read.

"Here's one," she said out loud. "Scott and Perkins. Her father is president of First Chicago Investments. And here's another one. Carruthers and St. James. Her father is Warren Carruthers of Carruthers, Trent and Stone."

"So, now that you have the names, what are you going to do?"

Elise looked up at her best friend, Dona Winters, and smiled. "What are *we* going to do," she corrected. "You're going to help me with this."

"I bake cakes, Elise."

"Not just cakes," she replied. "Incredibly romantic confections, masterpieces wrought from flour and eggs. That cake you baked for the Welton wedding was so beautiful it brought tears to my eyes. Those precious sugar-paste rosebuds and the ivy-leaf garland. Four tiers of exquisite beauty." For a moment, Elise lost herself in the memory of the Weltons' cake. The Welton affair had been such a lovely wedding, her best effort yet.

But she was well aware that's what she said about every wedding she'd planned, from the day she opened her wedding consulting business, right up to the nuptials she coordinated last Saturday. Each wedding was more special and more romantic than the last, each bride more perfect, each groom more dashing.

Elise's firm, A Tasteful Affair, was gaining recognition in Chicago, but the process was slow. Over the past three years, she had built a respectable portfolio of weddings, but she had yet to land a big one. A Gold Coast wedding. A wedding that combined a Chicago high-society bride and groom, a stellar guest list, visibility in the media and an unlimited budget.

"So how are my cakes going to help your business?"

"I figure we'll make some miniature wedding cakes, package each of them up in a pretty box and have them hand-delivered to the young ladies on this list. We'll put my business card inside the box. Then, a few days later, I'll make a follow-up call."

"That's not a bad idea. I think it might work."

"It'd better work. If I don't take on a few more clients in the next couple of months, I'm in serious trouble. This house might just come crashing down around me, and my business right along with it."

This house. Her house now. When her father and new stepmother had moved to Florida, they had happily turned the title to the crumbling Victorian town house over to Elise. The three-story brick house, located in Chicago's trendy Old Town neighborhood, had been the only home Elise had known and she was thrilled to have it for her own. The spacious first-floor parlor, with its huge bay window overlooking the street, made a perfect office. The dining room directly behind the parlor made a convenient workroom. And the lovely mahogany dining table served as a large work area, covered with sample books of wedding invitations, cakes and floral arrangements.

She had redecorated the house to match her romantic nature, in rich Victorian florals of muted rose and green. Every surface, from the walls to the tables to the floors, displayed a carefully calculated clutter, giving the rooms a warm, cozy feeling.

She always felt closer to her mother in these surroundings. Maybe that's why she was so determined to keep the house.

Elise's mother had also been a romantic at heart, taking pleasure in life's sweet and pretty moments. She had died nearly seventeen years before, when Elise was sixteen. Martin Sinclair had been devastated by his wife's death and for years Elise had wondered if her father would ever recover. But she had felt compelled to stay near him, so she gave up her dreams of going to New York to study art and instead completed a degree in design at Northwestern. She continued to live at home, keeping the household running as her father spent more and more time out of town on business. She suspected that he simply couldn't bear to be in a house that brought back memories of the wife he had cherished, yet he wouldn't consider selling it.

Then five years ago he had met Dorthi. They'd married after a short courtship and Elise had made plans to move out of the town house. But to her surprise, her father announced his retirement and within weeks he and Dorthi moved to Florida, leaving Elise with ownership of the house in exchange for sole custody of Dorthi's two prized Persian cats, Clorinda and Thisbe.

"The Girls," as Dorthi called them, were now sprawled across Elise's desk, taking one of their customary catnaps. Though Elise loved animals, she barely tolerated the presence of these two felines. They were fussy and aloof and selfish. And with their squished-in noses, Elise considered them the ugliest cats she'd ever seen.

Elise grabbed the drowsing Clorinda and unceremoniously set her on the floor. The fluffy white cat glared at her and with a sniff walked out of the room, her tail swishing haughtily. Thisbe, who never let Clorinda out of her sight, followed, shooting Elise a menacing glare as she left the room. Elise had learned to bear their hostility by reminding herself they were only cats.

"What about that mailing you did last month for corporate parties?" Dona inquired, a note of concern in her voice. "Did you have any response on that?"

"Out of one hundred sent, not one response. I made follow-up calls, but most of the companies were already dealing with an event planner. So much for my attempt to diversify."

"Hmm. Too bad." Dona paused, then rubbed her arms through her bulky knit sweater. "Is it cold in here, or is it just me?"

"No, it's cold in here. The boiler is on the fritz again." Elise walked over to the radiator and touched it. It was barely warm. Outside, a damp January wind rattled at the multipaned windows, each gust sending drafts of cold air though the sash to stir the lace curtains. "Great. I've got a new client due in ten minutes and this place is beginning to feel like a meat locker. A beautifully decorated Victorian meat locker."

"Why don't you get the boiler fixed?" Dona asked innocently.

"For the same reason I don't get the leaky roof fixed and for the same reason I'm two months behind on my utility bills. I need more clients. I hope this Jordan Prentiss decides to book with me. If it's a big affair, it would sure help my financial situation. You took the message. Does that name ring a bell with you?"

Dona shook her head. "I just assumed she was already a client, so I didn't ask questions."

"I know I've heard the name before. You'd think I'd remember." Elise shrugged and glanced at her watch. "Miss Prentiss is due in ten minutes and I've got to get this house warmed up."

"Well, I have to go." Dona grabbed her jacket and hurried to the door. "Call me tonight. We can get together and watch a video, maybe order a pizza."

"Only if we can watch *Indiscreet*. I just love that movie."

"We watched that last month," Dona protested.

"I know, but a girl can never have too much Cary Grant. And it's such a romantic movie."

"I'll think about it," Dona called from the hallway. "See you later."

Elise heard the door close behind her friend, then rushed over to the fireplace. She quickly added newspaper, kindling and two logs to the grate, then touched a match to the paper and watched as the flames licked at the logs. A nice roaring fire would add the perfect ambience to her meeting with Miss Prentiss. And it would also take the nip of winter out of the air.

She hurried through the foyer to the stairway. There was just enough time to change from her faded blue jeans and baggy sweatshirt before Miss Prentiss arrived. But her swift trip up to her third-floor bedroom was cut short by the sight of Thisbe. The smoke-gray cat sat with her nose pressed against the bottom of the front door.

"I'm not going to let you out," Elise scolded. "You're not an outside cat."

Thisbe looked up at her and meowed, then scratched at the door.

"Don't you remember what happened to Clorinda when she snuck out? She came back covered with grime and had a big scratch across her nose. Cats of your careful breeding do not socialize with street cats." Elise looked around the foyer. "Speaking of Clorinda, where is the little tramp?"

Thisbe scratched at the door again and let out an insistent howl. Elise's stomach tightened and her heart stopped. Oh, no! Clorinda must have snuck out when Dona left. If anything happened to one of "The Girls" her stepmother would never forgive her.

Elise grabbed a jacket from the hall closet, then ran to the kitchen and opened a can of tuna fish, letting the can rotate twice before releasing the lever on the electric can opener. The familiar humming sound brought Thisbe running for dinner, but there was no Clorinda. Elise ran back to the foyer and slipped out the front door. The cat couldn't have gotten far. Dona had left just minutes before.

Elise called Clorinda's name a few times before she got down on her hands and knees at the far edge of the house and crawled though the thick, leafless bushes that lined the front facade. This was where she'd found the runaway cat the last time. But this time the ground was soft and soggy from a brief winter thaw, and after only a few minutes, her hands were coated with mud.

"Here, kitty, kitty, kitty. Come on out, Clorinda." Elise waved the can of tuna through the air. Clorinda was a glutton for Chicken-of-the-Sea. She'd never be able to resist. Elise pushed through the heavy growth, cursing the entire feline species as the branches snapped back against her face like stinging whips and tangled in her hair. She reached the front stoop without finding a trace of the wayward cat.

Sliding though a small opening in the tall shrubbery, she grabbed the ornate cast-iron railing on the front steps, then pulled herself up and away from the clutching branches. As she brushed her hair out of her eyes, she realized someone was waiting on her front step.

A man stood with his back to her, stamping his feet against the cold. The wind ruffled his dark hair, brushing it against his collar. His wide shoulders were clearly outlined by the luxurious navy cashmere topcoat he wore.

"Can I help you?" she asked, shivering as a gust of wind swept past her.

He slowly turned around. His pale-blue eyes widened slightly upon seeing her. "I'm Jordan Prentiss. I have a two o'clock appointment with Elise Sinclair." He didn't smile, just looked at her, a tiny frown furrowing his brow. "I believe this is the right address." He pulled a piece of paper from his coat pocket and showed it to her.

Elise glanced down at the paper. This was Jordan Prentiss? This incredibly gorgeous, solitary man standing at her front door? On occasion, her clients would bring along their fiancés, but in most cases, the bride's mother or sister or best friend would be present.

Feeling more than a little self-conscious, Elise pulled herself over the railing and landed next to him on the stoop. In her haste to straighten her jacket, the can of tuna fish slipped from her hand, tumbled through the air and spattered over the shiny polish on his shoes. Mortified, she stared down at the oily mess for a long moment, then glanced up at him apologetically.

"Tuna fish," she mumbled and bent to brush the smelly goop off his shoes. Nervously she stood and, without thinking, held out her mud-caked hand. "It's a pleasure to meet you, Mr. Prentiss. I'm Elise Sinclair," she managed to blurt out.

He reached to take her hand, but at the last moment, she pulled it away. Blushing profusely, she gave a wan smile. "Mud," she explained, wiping her hands on her jeans.

Elise groaned inwardly. Jordan Prentiss had obviously come with the thought of using her consulting service, but with the way things were going, she would be lucky if he even stepped through her door.

As she sheepishly glanced up at his handsome features, a spark of recognition teased at her memory. Jordan Prentiss. Suddenly she realized where she had heard the name before—and seen the face. Jordan Prentiss, one of Chicago's most eligible. Man-about-town. Wealthy businessman and philanthropist. So, what was he doing on her front stoop? Alone?

His voice interrupted her scattered thoughts.

"It's cold out here. Do you think we could move inside?"

Elise smiled at him and pushed open the door, allowing him to enter. "I'm sorry. Please, come in." She took one last hurried look for Clorinda before closing the door, then turned to him.

"Have I come at a bad time?" he asked. His voice was soft and rich, but a bit icy around the edges.

"Of course not. I was just looking for my cat." Elise motioned for him to follow her into the parlor and indicated a chintz-covered sofa. "Please, sit down. Would you like to take off your coat?"

She watched Jordan shrug out of the topcoat and toss it across the back of the sofa. He was dressed in a finely tailored suit, also navy, with a blindingly white shirt and a red silk paisley tie.

The absence of the standard fiancée on his arm all but ruled out wedding plans. Could he be here on behalf of his daughter? He appeared to be in his mid-thirties, not old enough to have a daughter of marriageable age. Her confusion deepened. Maybe he wanted her to plan a corporate party. She tried to recall whether she had contacted his company and was nearly certain that she hadn't. She couldn't even recall the name of his company.

Why was he here? And why was he standing there, staring at her in such a puzzling fashion?

"Can I get you a cup of coffee, or maybe some tea?" Elise offered, hoping that he would refuse and she could move on to the next question—the question of what he wanted from her.

"No…thank you," Jordan answered, his gaze locked on her face. He opened his mouth to continue and she waited, offering him an encouraging smile. Finally he spoke, his voice detached, his expression composed. "You have something on your face." He reached out to brush his index finger along her cheek.

She felt a shiver run through her at his touch and wondered why she would have such a reaction when the room suddenly seemed so warm. He pulled his hand back and held out his finger. His fingertip was muddy.

Oh, no! She reached up and rubbed her cheeks furiously. Her fingers came back dirty. Then her hands swept to her hair and she heard the unmistakable crunch of dry leaves. "I—I was looking for my cat. She got out. Oh, I must look a mess." Beneath the mud, she could feel her cheeks flushing to a crimson shade.

A small smile quirked the corners of Jordan's mouth, but it quickly vanished and she wondered if she had only imagined it. "No, you look fine," he insisted, his voice the model of reserved politeness. "You just have a few smudges on your cheeks."

"If you'll excuse me, I'll just go clean up. Please, sit down and relax. I'll only be a moment."

She waited until Jordan had settled onto the overstuffed couch, then hurried from the room and ran up the stairs to her bedroom. The mirror above her dresser reflected her disheveled appearance.

Just a smudge? Dry leaves and tiny twigs clung to her strawberry-blond hair, framing her dirty face. She looked like something out of *A Midsummer Night's Dream.* There was no time to shower, so she brushed the debris from her hair, snatched a clean towel from the rack, wrapped it around her head and scrubbed her face clean. She would have to forgo makeup. There was no time. Jordan Prentiss did not look like a man to be kept waiting.

Elise dressed quickly, yanking on panty hose and shimmying into a pale-green sweater dress. She searched frantically for her ivory shoes. When she realized she had left them downstairs beneath her desk, she pulled another pair from her closet, slipped into them and stumbled from the room.

Nervous anticipation fluttered in her stomach as she slowly descended the steps. She took a deep breath to calm herself.

JORDAN CASUALLY surveyed his surroundings, amazed by the disconcerting clutter. The floral patterns of the couch, wallpaper and rug clashed in a riotous outcry of decorating madness. Added to the cacophony of color and pattern was an annoying variety of bric-a-brac scattered about the room and embellishing the walls. How could someone function in these surroundings?

His own office was spare and modern, each piece of furniture functional and adorned with only utilitarian accoutrements. His co-op on East Lake Shore Drive was the same, serenely clean and elegantly urban, leather and glass and tile, calming neutral colors.

This was definitely a place only a woman could love. A frivolous, feminine woman like Elise Sinclair.

Despite her baffling behavior, it had been immediately clear that beauty lurked behind her mud-streaked mask. The dirt couldn't hide the striking cheekbones or the wide, sensuous mouth. And her hair was the color of spun gold touched with copper, falling about her face in a tousled mess. She was soft and curvy in all the right places. He remembered her hand as she brushed it over her cheek, long, slender fingers and perfect pink nails.

Jordan blinked hard, startled by the direction of his thoughts. What had gotten into him, carrying on over a woman like that? Elise Sinclair wasn't even his type. He had always been attracted to women with a hard edge who accepted his pragmatic attitude toward relationships beyond the physical. Elise Sinclair didn't have a hard edge on her; she was all woman, with a vulnerability that was reflected in her liquid green eyes. The kind of woman every man wants for his wife.

Except him.

Jordan felt something brush against his leg and he looked down to find two cats at his feet, staring up at him with round amber eyes. Though he made no overt invitation, the cats leaped up onto the couch and settled themselves on either side of him, purring contentedly.

Cats. What had he expected? A big, bruising German shepherd? Or a yapping poodle? No, cats suited Elise Sinclair. He reached out to stroke the white cat on his left, scratching behind its ears. Birds would also be her style. Canaries or parakeets in brilliant colors and singing sweetly.

"I'm sorry to be so—"

Jordan turned to see Elise standing in the doorway, her face freshly scrubbed and rosy pink. She was staring at the cats, her gaze darting back and forth between the two furry creatures and Jordan.

"Where did you find her?" she asked.

"Is this the missing cat?"

She nodded.

"I didn't find her," Jordan replied. "She found me."

Elise narrowed her eyes and shot the white cat a venomous look.

"Are they not supposed to be on the furniture?" he asked.

Elise smiled, and Jordan relaxed a bit as he felt the warmth penetrate his icy composure.

"No, they're always on the furniture. They think the furniture in this house exists solely for their enjoyment. It's just that those cats don't like anyone. Not even me, and I feed them. In the five years that I've known them, they have never shown me, or anyone else for that matter, an ounce of affection." Elise sat down on the couch next to Jordan and tipped the gray cat's chin up to look into the animal's hooded eyes. "I wonder if they're sick."

The cat responded with a nasty hiss and a swipe of its paw, before indolently closing its eyes again.

"They appear to be quite healthy," Jordan said solemnly.

"You wouldn't want to take these cats home with you, would you?" she joked. "They seem to have taken a real liking to you."

"No," Jordan answered. "I'm not much of a . . . cat person."

"I didn't think so," she murmured, her attempt at levity ignored. She primly folded her hands in her lap and looked at him. "Well, Mr. Prentiss. What can I do for you?"

"I'd like you to plan my wedding." For a fleeting second, Jordan thought he saw disappointment shade her face, but then she smiled widely, her heart-shaped mouth curving up at the corners.

"I would love to help you plan your wedding. Why don't we set up a time for you and your fiancée to come in and discuss the preliminaries?"

"I'd like to take care of that right now, if that's agreeable with you."

"But wouldn't you rather have your bride here to participate in some of the decision making? It is her wedding, too."

Jordan stared at her for a moment before he spoke. "My...bride and I have discussed the matter...and she has agreed to let me make all the arrangements. With your help, of course. When decisions must be made, I will discuss them with her and pass along her wishes."

"This is most unusual, Mr. Prentiss. A woman's wedding day is the most important day of her life. Are you sure your fiancée wouldn't be happier working with me directly? If she can't, perhaps her mother or her sister would agree to help."

"Miss Sinclair, there will be a great deal of attention focused on this wedding. I do not want my fiancée exposed to any undue pressure or inconvenience. If you have a problem with this, I'm sure I can—"

"Oh, no, Mr. Prentiss," she interrupted, a conciliatory smile on her lips. "Whatever you and your fiancée have decided is fine with me."

"We want a large, traditional wedding. I would expect approximately four hundred guests." He saw Elise's eyes widen with shock. "Of course, you will have an unlimited budget for the wedding. Whatever you feel is appropriate is fine with me...and my fiancée," he added quickly. "But you must be extremely discreet in making your plans. I do not want anyone learning of this wedding until the invitations are sent. Can you do that, Miss Sinclair?"

Elise nodded mutely.

"Then you accept the job?"

"Yes...yes, I accept."

"Good." Jordan stood up and extended his hand. Elise slowly rose and took it. "I look forward to working with you, Miss Sinclair. Now, I really must be going." He reached into his breast pocket, withdrew a business card and handed it to her. "If you have any questions, just call me. But most of the decisions I leave up to you. I trust your judgment on these matters. Send me whatever papers I need to sign along with an invoice for your expected expenses and charges and I'll be sure you are compensated immediately."

Jordan nodded to her, effectively ending their meeting, then picked up his coat and walked into the foyer. She followed a few steps behind him.

"Wait. You can't leave yet. We have so many more things to discuss."

Her hand touched his elbow and Jordan turned to her with a questioning look. When she snatched her fingers away, he felt a strange sensation of loss.

"Have you chosen a date for the wedding?" she asked.

"April 18."

She relaxed and smiled in relief. "That gives us plenty of time. That's over a year away."

"This April 18."

"Three months from now?" Her voice betrayed a hint of alarm. "You want me to plan a wedding for four hundred guests in three months?"

"Is that a problem?"

She looked at him, astonished, then covered her expression carefully. "No. I'm sure I can take care of it. But wouldn't you rather have a June wedding? April can be such a terrible month for weather. And June would give us a little more time to plan."

"The wedding date is set, Miss Sinclair," Jordan said as he pulled on his coat. "It must be April 18."

She sighed in resignation. "Have you made *any* plans? Have you booked a location for the reception?"

"Isn't that part of your job?"

At first she seemed put off by his curt reply, but her expression of dismay was quickly replaced by one of cool efficiency. "I'll work up some budget figures for you and take care of finding a place for the reception. Why don't we plan to meet later this week to go over the preliminary plans. Would Friday be all right?"

"Fine. Call my secretary and set up a time. I'll let her know to expect your call." Jordan opened the front door. "Goodbye, Miss Sinclair."

"Goodbye, Mr. Prentiss."

Jordan pulled the door shut behind him and scanned the narrow street for his driver and limousine. As he stepped into the car, he looked back at the house. Though the fussy decor had made him uncomfortable at first, he had sensed a certain warmth and contentment sitting in Elise's flower-strewn parlor. He had been tempted to stay longer, but had found his mind wandering from the wedding plans and lingering on Elise Sinclair's beautiful features.

As the limo pulled away from the curb, Jordan made another instant business decision. He would not turn over plans for the wedding to Pete Stockton. It would look too suspicious, and Elise was already questioning the absence of the bride. No, Jordan would work with her personally.

He smiled to himself as he realized that this was the only business decision he had made all day that gave him the slightest bit of pleasure.

2

SEVENTEEN BRIDESMAIDS, not to mention the junior attendants. All of them dressed in a different color. Purple, pink, pumpkin, periwinkle. It would be laughable, a disaster of catastrophic proportions. Like an explosion in a paint factory.

"Seventeen bridesmaids? I've never planned a wedding with that many attendants." Elise groped for a gentle way to dissuade the bride. "A wedding party that size could be very . . . unmanageable." She had wanted to say ostentatious or even tacky. But brides were a very unstable breed and one wrong word could result in torrents of tears. "There may not be room for all of them at the front of the church."

"Then we'll get a bigger church," Minny chirped. "There is no way I can leave any of my friends out. *No way*. They would hate me forever and I just couldn't stand that. Besides, Daddy said I could have whatever I wanted and this is what I want."

"All right," Elise said patiently. "But why don't we rethink the color scheme. With that many attendants, it might be best to choose one color for the bridesmaids' dresses." She hesitated, considering how an art-deco wedding might look. But seventeen bridesmaids standing at the front of a church in black would probably resemble a flock of crows perched on a phone line. A snowball wedding would be just as bad, enough white to send the guests home blinded by the sight.

"How about having all the girls in emerald green? Or deep magenta?"

"But I really, really wanted a rainbow wedding," Minny whined. "Mother, tell her."

Elise looked to Grace Marbury, long-suffering wife of Crazy Bill Marbury, Chicago's king of discount appliances. Though Grace had endeavored to inject a bit of class into her daughter's wedding, her every suggestion had been overruled by Minny and her indulgent daddy. Grace smiled at Elise and shrugged. It was clear she had given up the fight long ago. Maybe it was about time for Elise to throw in the monogrammed tea towel, too.

No, Elise scolded herself, there was a wedding at stake, along with her reputation. She had to give it one last try.

"With a rainbow wedding, you have to be very careful how you assign the colors," Elise began, fixing a deeply concerned look on her face. "What if someone doesn't like the color you've chosen for her? What if she wants the color you've chosen for someone else? If you give the best colors to your best friends, how will your other attendants feel? They might really, *really* be mad at you. Wouldn't it be best to choose your favorite color? After all, it is your wedding."

Elise could see the wheels turning in Minny's head as she weighed this new dilemma. Finally the girl sighed dejectedly.

"All right, we'll dress them all in one color, even though I think it's really, really boring. But it's got to be purple, 'cause that's my absolute favorite color. Do you think tuxedos come in lavender? Wouldn't that look cool—purple dresses and lavender tuxedos? And we could even dye those boring white roses purple."

"Purple would be lovely, Minny." Elise unclenched her hands and relaxed her jaw. She had won the day's battle, but she knew she was losing the war. After the Marbury wedding, she might be forced to change the name of her business to A Taste*less* Affair. "We'll discuss the men's colors next week. Let me know when you'd like to shop for the bridesmaids' dresses and we'll choose something stunning for the girls. Usually the bridesmaids accompany the bride on the shopping trip, but I think seventeen girls would make it impossible to come to a decision."

"Oh, no. We have to take them all along. I promised. If I don't, they'll hate me forever."

Elise stood up and walked the Marburys to the front door, collapsing against it after she shut it behind them. At times like these she wondered what had possessed her to get into the wedding business at all. Why hadn't she followed her childhood dream of becoming a bus driver? Or a princess? Or a cowgirl? Any one of those careers would have been better than what she had chosen.

If she hadn't desperately needed the income from the Marbury wedding, she would never have taken the job. But Crazy Bill had deep pockets, bottomless pockets when it came to his only daughter. Thank God she had the Prentiss wedding to outweigh the Marbury debacle. An unlimited budget and little interference from the bride or the groom. She would plan a wedding the likes of which Chicago had never seen.

Elise glanced at the clock on the mantel. She was due at Jordan Prentiss's office in an hour for their first planning meeting. The cab ride downtown during the afternoon rush could take half that time. She ran up the stairs to change, a hum of anticipation pulsing in her head. After their last meeting, she wanted to look her best. But she stopped midway up the second flight of stairs with a sudden realization.

She was worrying about her appearance like a lovesick teenager! Jordan was an engaged man. Elise slowly sat down on the stairs, winding her fingers around a pair of balusters and resting her forehead between them.

She was attracted to him. From the moment she saw him standing on her front stoop, she had felt an undeniable connection, a tiny current that drew her to him. His image had drifted through her thoughts over and over during the past four days and she had found herself fantasizing about the feel of his soft, dark hair and the touch of his finely sculpted lips.

But it was his eyes that had drawn her to him, his unsettling habit of looking directly into her gaze as if he could see her soul. Though he maintained the outward appearance of a cool, detached businessman, she'd noticed something more simmering beneath the surface. It was as if the man on the outside was a careful affectation to cover the man inside. And the only hint of the inner man had been in the eyes. Those stunning pale-blue eyes. A boyish, almost innocent feature on such a sophisticated and worldly man.

What had she seen in those eyes? Her first impression had been doubt. But he was such a confident man; nothing could rattle that ironclad composure. Pain? Elise let the thought swirl in her mind. Romantic images of a long-lost love, a broken promise, a man betrayed drifted through her thoughts.

Elise shook her head. She was letting her imagination run away with her again. Why did she always try to romanticize life? Jordan Prentiss was probably an ordinary man with ordinary problems. Maybe he had stubbed his toe as he'd gotten out of bed that morning or maybe his fiancée was driving him crazy as brides had a tendency to do. Or maybe the stock market was down.

She had attached a mystique to the man, then let her fantasies take over. It hadn't been the first time. Elise had an amazing knack for stumbling upon tortured souls. Every man she had dated boasted a painful past. And those who didn't, well, she managed to invent one for them. Then she threw herself into healing them with love and affection. And when they were healed, Elise found herself with an ordinary man and his ordinary problems, not the romantic, happily-ever-after hero she had hoped for. The infatuation would die and Elise would be left with just another name to add to her list of male "friends." At last count, she had more male friends than Minny Marbury had bridesmaids.

Elise sighed. She had let her fantasies about Jordan Prentiss go too far. It was no wonder. Jordan was an incredibly attractive man, probably the most handsome man she had ever met. He exuded an air of tightly leashed sensuality, carefully controlled and hidden behind his indifferent facade.

She would have to put a stop to her crazy infatuation—they were very unprofessional feelings for a wedding consultant to have toward her client. Though unrequited love was a very romantic notion, she was sensible enough to know that it could only lead to heartache.

Elise raised her head and looked up the stairs to see Clorinda and Thisbe staring down their ugly noses at her from the third-floor landing. "Oh, what do you know?" Elise shouted, sending the pair scurrying for the safety of the linen closet. "If you're not careful, I may accidentally leave the front door open and you'll both find yourselves eating out of garbage cans and associating with alley cats on a permanent basis."

A half hour later she was seated in the back of a cab, weaving through traffic on Division Street, dressed in a simple suit topped with a conservative wool trench coat. She had decided that dressing to attract the attention of Jordan Prentiss would only be inviting trouble, so she had even gone so far as to pull back her wavy hair into a simple businesslike knot at her nape.

The cab dropped her off in front of an impressive glass-and-steel high rise on the east side of Michigan Avenue near Water Tower Place. She gave the security guard Jordan's card, and after he confirmed her appointment, she was directed to a bank of elevators. The elevator opened on the twenty-third floor and Elise found herself facing the wide glass doors of the corporate headquarters of BabyLove Baby Foods. The company name was painted on each door in gleaming silver script wrapped around the familiar BabyLove logo, a heart-shaped silver spoon.

Elise stepped into the reception area and a pretty young woman behind a circular desk greeted her with a smile.

"Good evening, Miss Sinclair," she said as she stood up.

"Good evening. I'm here to see Mr. Prentiss. We have a five-thirty appointment."

"Mr. Prentiss is just finishing up a meeting. He asked that I show you back to his office."

Elise followed the receptionist down a wide hallway. The woman pushed open a pair of mahogany doors at the end of the hall and stepped aside to let Elise through.

The corner office was huge and starkly modern. A wide glass-topped table served as a desk and two sleek leather guest chairs sat before it, with a more imposing desk chair behind it. Two of the four walls were solid glass, with the interiors of the offices across Michigan Avenue visible through the tinted windows. The other two walls were adorned with large postimpressionist paintings.

Elise recognized the artists immediately and wondered what paintings of museum quality were doing in the office of the president of a baby-food company. If Jordan was a collector of art, he had very good taste. But it was hard to believe that the taciturn businessman she had met four days ago would collect art for its beauty alone. A man like Jordan Prentiss was more apt to collect art for its investment value.

"Could I get you anything to drink, Miss Sinclair?" the receptionist asked.

Elise shook her head. "No, thank you."

"Then I'll let Mr. Prentiss know you're here."

She walked from the office, closing the doors behind her. Elise placed her briefcase beside one of the chairs, slipped out of her coat, and draped it over the arm, then strolled over to the windows. The twinkling lights from the rush-hour traffic outlined the street below as the cars, cabs and buses crawled home from the Loop on Michigan Avenue.

"Hello, dear."

Elise spun around to find a plump white-haired woman standing before her. She was smiling, her eyes sparkling behind wire-rimmed glasses and her face alight with undisguised curiosity. She wore an elegant pink suit with pearl buttons down the front of the jacket. Elise wondered how she had managed to enter the room without making a sound then looked down at her shoes. A pair of high-tops completed her outfit.

"Hello," Elise replied. "I was just waiting for Mr. Prentiss."

"You're here for Jordan? You must be Elise." The woman walked to Jordan's desk and carefully flipped through his calendar. "I'm sorry Jordan has kept you waiting. He sometimes gets so involved in business matters that he forgets the time." She began to sort through the file folders on his desk, peeking inside one every so often, then putting it carefully back in place before continuing her search.

So this was Jordan's secretary, Elise thought. Somehow she had imagined Jordan with a much younger, more coldly efficient woman, not someone who looked like everyone's favorite grandmother.

"I suppose you're here to discuss the wedding," the woman said, engrossed in the contents of a large white envelope.

"You know about the wedding?" Elise asked.

The older woman smiled, the corners of her eyes and mouth crinkling into deep grooves, as if smiling were the predominant expression on her face and had been her whole life. "Of course I do, dear. I'm well aware of what Edward's been stirring up. Although I can't say that I approve of Jordan's plans. I would hate to see him in an unhappy marriage. What do you think?"

"About what?"

"Why, Jordan's happiness, of course," she replied, acting as if Elise should know exactly what she was talking about. "He takes on too much and now this."

"This?"

"Yes, this. What are we going to do about that boy, Elise?"

"I—I'm not sure I know what you mean."

The woman reached out and patted Elise on the hand. "I'm sure you don't, at least not yet. But you will, my dear, you'll see. I'm counting on it."

The woman gave her a cheerful wave and bustled out of the room, leaving Elise with a sense of utter confusion. What had she meant by her cryptic statements? She'd mentioned Jordan as a little boy. Would his secretary have known him as a child? And her words had almost implied that she was against Jordan's marriage, that it would cause him unhappiness. And who was Edward? Elise was still staring at the doorway in befuddlement when Jordan walked in.

"Miss Sinclair," he greeted, stepping to her and shaking her hand in a firm, impersonal manner. "I'm sorry to keep you waiting. I hope Kay made you comfortable."

"Comfortable" was hardly the word for it. In fact, her conversation with Jordan's secretary had made her quite uncomfortable.

"My secretary was out sick today so I had Kay stay at the front desk until you arrived. Did she offer you something to drink? Coffee or tea, perhaps?"

"No," Elise answered, quickly covering her confusion. If Jordan's secretary was sick, who was the sweet little woman she'd encountered just minutes ago in his office? She seemed quite at ease shuffling through the papers on Jordan's desk. And she was obviously close to Jordan—she knew about the wedding.

"No, she didn't offer you anything?"

"No . . . I mean yes, she did, and no, I don't need anything," Elise replied, stumbling over her words and glancing up at him. He was gazing at her in that same intense way she remembered from their encounter in her parlor, as if he were trying to read her thoughts.

He was as handsome as she recalled. His hair was dark brown, nearly black, and was combed neatly back. She imagined it windblown and falling in waves over his forehead, imagined him with a cheerful, boyish smile instead of his usual cool, prepossessed expression. But right now the only clues to his state of mind were a questioning arch of his eyebrow and a tiny upturn of the corners of his firm lips, not nearly enough to constitute a smile. She found herself blushing slightly.

"Well," he said, "why don't we get started, then?"

He took his place behind his desk and Elise sat down in one of the guest chairs, grabbed her briefcase and extracted a file folder and pen. She looked up at him and found him staring out the window. Elise cleared her throat and waited for him to turn to her.

"I'm listening," he said softly, toying with a small jar he had pulled off his credenza.

"All right," she replied. "First of all, I'll need your full name as well as your fiancée's."

Jordan paused for a moment, staring at the baby food jar he held in his hands. "Jordan Broderick Prentiss."

Watching his long, slender fingers grip the glass, she tried to imagine what his hands might feel like touching her. She bit her lower lip, disturbed by the direction of her thoughts, and hastily scribbled the name on her file form. Then she paused, her pen poised, and listened for the next name. "And your fiancée's?" she prompted.

"Is that necessary?" Jordan asked, directing a cool blue gaze at her.

"The fiancée or the name? It's usually standard practice to have a fiancée if one plans to get married. As for her name, if I'm to order invitations, it would definitely help." Elise shifted uncomfortably in her chair, realizing her answer sounded mildly sarcastic. But why was he so secretive about the bride's identity? First, there was his insistence on the April wedding date, and now, his reluctance to give her a simple name. What possible reason could there be for all this subterfuge?

The reason came to her like a bolt from the blue. Jordan's bride was a celebrity! In his much-publicized bachelor days, he had dated his fair share of famous women, she had learned, including several well-known movie actresses and a famous pop singer. That could be the only reason for attempting to keep the bride's name out of the press. What a chivalrous gesture, Elise thought with a smile. It was the first spark of romanticism she had seen from the aloof Mr. Prentiss.

What a delicious thought! Jordan Prentiss, white knight, protecting his lady fair. But why the quick wedding? Maybe the future Mrs. Prentiss had to get back to Hollywood. Or maybe she had a concert tour coming up. Or maybe . . . she was pregnant. Oh, dear, a high-society shotgun wedding. She stopped herself. Her imagination was running rampant again.

Still, if Jordan Prentiss really was marrying a celebrity, this wedding would bring her the kind of publicity she had only dreamed of. The front page of the society section. Society brides fighting for her services. What did she care whether the bride was pregnant or not?

But she *did* care.

"You'll just have to put off ordering the invitations for now," Jordan said.

Elise nodded reluctantly. She could wait for the name, but she would get it out of him sooner or later. "We can put off ordering them for at least another month, and if you're willing to pay a bit extra, another two months."

"As I told you earlier, Miss Sinclair, money is no object."

"Yes. Well, then, I'm sure the invitations will be no problem. Next, we need to discuss the location for the reception. Since you are firm on your wedding date as April 18..." She paused, hoping he might offer an explanation for the early date, but not really expecting a straightforward reply.

"Yes," he said. "April 18."

Her hope for a brief reprieve fell. "An evening reception is out of the question. All the hotels that can accommodate four hundred guests are booked. That, in turn, rules out an afternoon wedding. We could consider your country club, if you have one."

Jordan shook his head. "No country club."

"Or your home or family estate."

He shook his head again. "No room."

"I did happen upon one bit of luck, though. The Drake had a cancellation in their Gold Coast Room for the early afternoon of the eighteenth. It's the city's most elegant location. I would suggest a morning wedding with a champagne brunch following. Although that's not quite as traditional as you had hoped for, it would be acceptable given the time constraints."

"Fine," he answered. He looked over at her. "Is there anything else?"

She held back a gasp of shock. Did he think this
wedding was going to plan itself? Lord, the man could
be aggravating! "Yes, of course there is. I have a whole
list here. Are you sure you wouldn't rather have your
fiancée here to help?" she asked, wondering just how
far she could push the issue.

He looked down at the jar in his hand and opened it,
then swiveled the lid back and forth distractedly. "Go
on," he ordered, blatantly ignoring her question.

"Where do you plan to have the ceremony?" Elise
asked. This was an easy question, one she was certain
to get a solid answer for.

"A church," he replied. "That is where one is supposed to get married, isn't it?"

Elise ground her teeth. "Yes and no. Churches are
sometimes harder to schedule than receptions. If you
have a church of choice, I can check on the availability.
If not, you can hold the ceremony at the hotel."

"No, it has to be a church. My grandfather belonged
to Fourth Presbyterian. Try there."

Elise wrote the name of the church on her form.
Fourth Presbyterian was one of Chicago's most beautiful churches, a truly romantic spot for a wedding.
Elise could already picture the floral decorations she
would choose for the picturesque Gothic church, swags
of greenery and white satin ribbon decorating the
sanctuary and sprays of roses with candles at the end
of each pew. And a huge arrangement of her favorite
flowers, Casablanca lilies and white roses, adorning the
altar. It would be stunning, a wedding to remember for
years.

Elise drew herself back to the present and glanced up
at Jordan. Now they were getting somewhere. An ac-
tual decision had been made. "Fourth Presbyterian

would be perfect. And since most Protestant weddings are scheduled for the afternoon, the church might still be available at—" She silently watched him remove the lid of the jar he was playing with and hold it under his nose, sniffing at the contents. "This late—" He wasn't listening to anything she was saying. "Date." She might as well be planning a wedding for two mannequins in the window of Marshall Field's.

"As for the menu," she continued smoothly.

"Yes, the menu," he murmured, nodding. Suddenly, he set the jar down, turned to his computer and began tapping at the keys.

"Mr. Prentiss?" Elise watched his intent study of the screen. "Mr. Prentiss?" He made no move to resume their meeting.

"Fine," Elise muttered. "I'll just work on the menu while you do whatever it is you're doing. For the main course, I would suggest sardine sandwiches and grits. Of course, if you would prefer hot dogs, that's fine, but hot dogs don't have the same...oh, I don't know...panache as a good sardine sandwich." Jordan showed no reaction. "And for dessert, instead of cake, we could have cotton candy. Wait! I have a wonderful idea. We could dress the bride and groom as clowns and make this wedding a real circus."

The room was silent. Elise waited and wondered how long it would take for him to realize she had stopped speaking and return his attention to the wedding. Finally he looked up.

"I'm sorry, what were you saying?"

"We should discuss the color scheme," Elise replied evenly, hoping this would elicit more interest from him. "I would assume your bride has chosen her bridesmaids. What about the dresses for them?"

"No bridesmaids," Jordan responded.

No country club, no family estate, no bridesmaids. What was with this guy? "You mean no dresses?"

"No dresses and no bridesmaids."

No bridesmaids? What was a wedding without bridesmaids? Elise rubbed her temple, feeling one of her I-wish-I-drove-a-bus-for-a-living headaches coming on. Gee, maybe Minny Marbury could lend a few bridesmaids to the future Mr. and Mrs. Prentiss. Their wedding was promising to be much more bizarre than Minny's. "You have to at least have a maid of honor and a best man."

"I do—I mean, we do?" Jordan asked. He shrugged. "All right."

His sudden acquiescence surprised her. "Your bride and her honor attendant will need to go out and look for a bridesmaid's dress."

"Can you do that?"

"Of course, I do it all the time. But usually I'm accompanied by the bride."

"Well, you'll have to do it yourself."

Elise's frustration shot to the boiling point. If he gave her one more evasive or obtuse answer, she was sure she would scream. How was she supposed to plan a wedding with no cooperation from the bride or the groom? She had once thought their lack of interference would make her job easier, but now she was beginning to regret her earlier enthusiasm.

"All right," she said with practiced patience. "What is your bride's favorite color?"

Jordan paused.

"You don't know your fiancée's favorite color?" Elise calmed herself. She had learned that Jordan Prentiss cared little about this wedding, but now she was beginning to believe that he cared even less about his fiancée. She quickly reconsidered her opinion of the man before her. Chivalrous? Hah! He was quite possibly the most unromantic man she had ever met. It was a wonder he had even found a woman to agree to marry him and incomprehensible that the woman, pregnant or not, would have the romantic fortitude to put up with him for life. The image of a shotgun, pointed at his head, flashed through her mind.

"Black," he finally said, as if this was the only answer he was really sure of.

"Black," Elise repeated.

"Yes, she wears black all the time. I would assume it's her favorite color."

"Black is not an appropriate color for a morning wedding." Elise heard her voice rise several decibels. "Black is better suited to funerals."

"Hmm. Then it should be black," he muttered as he stared into the jar.

She watched in amazement as he stuck his finger inside and then put it in his mouth. He grimaced, turning in his chair to face her.

"Here, smell this." He reached over his desk and pushed the jar at her.

She drew away.

"Go ahead," he urged. "Smell it."

Elise sniffed at the contents of the little jar. "It doesn't smell like anything."

"Exactly," he replied, a note of triumph in his voice.

"Taste it." He dipped his index finger into the jar again and held it out to her. Without thinking, she drew his finger into her mouth. When he didn't pull his hand away, she looked at him with wide eyes, realizing just what she was doing. Slowly Elise pulled away, con-

scious of the erotic tingle that touched her lips and
tongue. He, too, seemed suddenly aware of what had
passed between them and hesitantly drew his fingers
away, letting his touch linger for just a moment on her
lower lip.

Elise let the taste of the baby food and his finger
mingle in her mouth before swallowing convulsively.
"It—it doesn't taste like anything."

"Precisely," he said, his voice low, his gaze locked
with hers. Then he shook himself out of his daze and
smiled.

A tiny thrill rippled through her as she watched the
corners of his mouth turn up in a charming grin.

"We know for a fact that babies can tell the difference between strained peas and banana pudding. Any
mother will tell you that. And if they're aware of that
difference, they probably differentiate between good
carrots and this tasteless orange mush we package as
carrots.

"The problem is in the canning process," he explained, pushing himself away from his desk to pace
before the windows. "We try to avoid the use of pre-
servatives, salt and sugar, cook the hell out of the food
and then grind it up. It ends up bland and tasteless.
Would you eat that?"

Elise shook her head, watching as he paced before
her.

"Then why would a baby?" he continued, not waiting for an answer. "I've been thinking about adding a
line of frozen, microwaveable baby foods to Baby-
Love. It's going to take a tremendous amount of investment in new processing and packaging equipment,
plus a big marketing and advertising budget, but we

could make baby food that tastes good. What do you think?"

She could hear the excitement in his voice, see the passion in his eyes, and she wondered whether that same burning passion she saw now had ever been directed toward his fiancée. She wondered what it would feel like to have that passion aimed at her. "I think it's a wonderful idea."

"My board of directors disagrees with you, me, and the research. Our research shows that ninety percent of our product is consumed in the home and eighty percent of our customers own microwaves. The only drawback to frozen microwaveable baby food is that it doesn't travel well. The board feels that this is enough to kill the idea. I think they're being stupidly short-sighted."

"Well, I think it's a brilliant idea. I'm surprised no one has thought of it before."

"Someone would have if babies could talk. They would have told us long ago why they feel compelled to spit up their dinners all over their parents' shoulders."

Elise giggled at Jordan's serious expression. Could it be that Jordan Prentiss had a sense of humor? Though he wasn't smiling, she could detect a hint of sardonic wit in his voice. It was a small chink in the impenetrable armor he hid behind and she felt as if she had been allowed a glimpse of the real man, a man she found utterly intriguing.

"Do you and your fiancée plan to have children after you're—" Elise stopped. The words had just popped out. The question was such a natural one, but combined with the evidence she had already gleaned about the future Mrs. Prentiss, she realized that it might appear overtly nosy. "—married?"

Jordan looked puzzled for a moment. "I don't know. We haven't discussed it. But yes, I think I would like to have children."

She stifled a sigh of relief and her mental picture of the shotgun disappeared in a puff of smoke. For some unknown reason, she was glad Jordan wasn't being forced into marriage. But then she realized the idea of a shotgun wedding was preposterous. Jordan Prentiss was not the kind of man to be forced into doing anything against his will.

"How many would you like?" Elise asked, regaining her composure.

"Two. Two would be best."

"Two sounds like a nice number. I was an only child, so two sounds like a good number to me." Once again, Elise's words escaped her mouth before checking in with her mind. What was she saying? "Not that I meant that you and I—I mean, me and my husband—when I find a husband, that is—after I'm married—I'd like two children, with my husband." Elise flushed.

Jordan grinned at her as he slid into his chair and studied her openly. "You changed your hair," he said, shifting the conversation in a manner that was becoming increasingly familiar to her. "I liked it the other way."

Elise reached out to touch her hair. "The other way?"

He motioned, waving his hand near his shoulder. "Down. Loose and curly. The way you had it the last time I saw you."

"Oh . . ." The word hung in the air between them. Elise's mind raced, wondering how they had gotten so far off the subject of the wedding. Her only excuse was that Jordan Prentiss was the oddest client she had ever had. And the most irresistible. Maybe all grooms are like this, she thought. It certainly explained why they were all getting married.

"I think we should get back to the wedding plans, Mr. Prentiss," she suggested.

"Jordan," he said, his gazed still locked on her. "You can call me 'Jordan' . . . Elise."

She liked the sound of her name on his lips, the way it sent a shiver skittering down her spine. "Jordan," she repeated, trying to calm her pounding heart. "Now, about the budget."

"What about the budget, Elise?"

"Three hundred per person should cover everything." She expected a reaction—shock, discomfort, disbelief. After all, she was proposing a total budget of $120,000. But his gaze never wavered from hers. "Of course that doesn't include the wedding dress."

"That sounds quite reasonable to me."

Reasonable? It was enough to buy the most lavish wedding Chicago had to offer and then some. Elise looked down at her notes, frantically searching for the next subject of discussion and thoroughly rattled by his outward show of calm. She glanced up and found him watching her intently. They stared at each other a long moment before she finally spoke.

"I—I think we've covered everything I need for now," she said, suddenly feeling an intense need to escape Jordan's magnetic presence. "I'll check on the church and I'll make arrangements to meet with the caterers at the Drake to discuss the menu. If you'd like to be involved with the choice of—"

"I'll be there," Jordan said, a crooked smile touching his lips. "Call my secretary with the time and date."

Elise stood up and pulled her coat from the chair beside her. She fumbled with her briefcase, then held out her hand to Jordan. "All right . . . fine . . . I guess that's it, then." She pulled her hand from Jordan's warm grip, the heat searing her palm. "I'll talk to you sometime next week, Mr.—er, Jordan."

Elise turned for the door. Jordan followed and pulled it open for her. "Good night," she mumbled as she brushed past him.

"Miss Sinclair?"

She turned back to him.

"Just one more thing. About this clown idea of yours . . ."

Elise felt her face flush. *Oh, no. He* had *been listening!*

"The idea has merit, especially the cotton candy for dessert. I'll give it some serious thought." He smiled again, this time a devastating, heart-stopping smile. "Good night."

JORDAN WATCHED her hasty departure down the long hallway and smiled to himself.

God, she was beautiful. Even in that button-down suit he could still make out the soft, lush form beneath—full breasts, a tiny waist, curvy hips and legs that wouldn't quit. Those eyes, like a cat, green and set at a slight upward tilt, and that mouth, full and expressive. There was no doubt about it. He wanted Elise Sinclair. The flicker of attraction he had felt at their first meeting had turned into a fire.

A fire he would have to snuff out.

In the past, it had always been a matter of control, a matter of containing the desire. As long as he was in absolute control of his basic urges, there was no chance that the relationship would go any farther than he wanted it to. He would not be swayed by lust and emotion. He would not make the same mistake his father had. He would not allow a woman to ruin his life.

He had never experienced a sexual attraction as deep and intense as he felt for Elise Sinclair—and as dangerous. Jordan drew a deep breath and attempted to smother the flames Elise had ignited. He would put her out of his mind.

Besides, having her was impossible now that he was an "engaged" man, he rationalized. Elise Sinclair did not seem the type to play fast and loose with her clients, or any man for that matter. She was more likely the kind of woman to give herself only to a man she loved, a man who loved her in return.

And Jordan could not be that man. An unexpected stab of disappointment twisted in his gut at the realization that she was the first woman he had ever truly wanted and the only woman he couldn't have.

"So that's Elise Sinclair. I can see why you decided to take me off the planning committee." Pete Stockton stood in the hallway, and had obviously enjoyed the same view of Elise's retreating form.

Jordan walked back into his office, with Pete at his heels. He slid into his chair and leaned back, closing his eyes and rubbing his forehead.

"How did it go?" Pete asked.

"Playing out this charade is a lot harder than I thought it would be," he said, his voice shadowed with exhaustion. "I've never been good at lying, especially to women. She is definitely suspicious. We have got to find a fiancée for me and fast." *The sooner I get engaged,* he thought to himself, *the sooner Elise Sinclair is forgotten.* "What about the party? Any responses from your list of five?"

"Even on such short notice, they're all planning to come. You don't throw many parties, but when you do, it's the hottest ticket in town. It should be quite an affair. Thirty-five of Chicago's richest and most powerful and five prospective brides, all seemingly gathered to salute your newest cause, the Children's Museum at the Art Institute. And, of course, I'll be there to help you out."

Jordan glanced at him. "Help me out?"

"You're going to need me, unless you plan on charming all five of them at the same time. I do respect your skills as a bachelor, but that's beyond even you. Somebody's got to pay court to four of them while you're interviewing the fifth. And if they bring guests, you'll need me to run interference."

"I don't think that's necessary. I'm sure I can handle the situation by myself."

Pete sat down across from Jordan. "May I speak candidly?"

"You've never asked my permission before. What's stopping you now?"

"Let's face it, Jordan. You're not exactly Mr. Romance. In fact, when it comes to matters of the heart, you haven't progressed beyond the Dark Ages. In order to make this plan work, you've got to convince a woman to marry you in less than two months, *before* the wedding invitations go out. You've never had a relationship with a woman that's lasted that long."

Jordan considered Pete's statement soberly. He was right. He'd heard the same accusation from nearly every woman he'd had a relationship with, short-lived though the association may have been. Women did not consider him romantic in the least. And he hadn't a clue as to what women did consider romantic. But Pete did.

"All right," Jordan muttered. "You can come. Are all the arrangements made?"

"The caterers will be at your place tomorrow by four. The party starts at eight. I've called your cleaning lady and she'll be in early tomorrow morning. All you need to do is show up. It's formal dress, by the way."

"I hate parties," he grumbled. "All that small talk drives me crazy. How long is this supposed to last?"

"Three hours, maybe four."

Jordan sighed and pushed himself out of his chair. "If it weren't for Edward, I wouldn't be in this mess. Anything new on him?"

"He met today with Cyril Carstairs. They had a very cozy lunch at Belle Maison. Edward had the veal and Cyril had a Caesar salad. The way I figure it, Cyril is the swing vote. He's the one you need to get to first. The others can wait."

Jordan opened his briefcase and began to toss file folders into it. "I'll call him Monday. Do you have the regional sales reports finished?"

Pete held out a file folder that he'd picked off of Jordan's desk. "Isn't it a little early for you to be leaving? It's only six o'clock. You're usually here until at least ten."

"I'll be in early tomorrow morning. We can go over the reports then." Jordan grabbed his coat from the closet.

"Do you want me to call your driver?"

"No, I think I'll walk home. I could use the exercise. See you tomorrow, Pete."

Jordan strode to the elevator, pulling on his coat and fishing in his pockets for his cashmere-lined leather gloves. As he pushed open the wide glass doors of the ground floor lobby and stepped outside, the wind that howled unceasingly between the buildings on Michigan Avenue hit him squarely in the chest. For a moment, he regretted the decision to walk. But thoughts of Elise still nagged at his mind and he would do anything, including walking in a subzero wind chill, to rid himself of this unwanted attraction for her.

The brisk ten-minute walk home along the lake did nothing to drive Elise's lovely face from his thoughts. The biting lake wind didn't dispel the heat that burned deep inside of him. The double scotch he had with his dinner didn't numb the uncomfortable craving he felt.

Jordan Prentiss would choose a bride in less than twenty-four hours, yet he fell asleep that night with an image of Elise Sinclair on his mind.

3

HER PERFECTLY MANICURED hand slithered down the front of Jordan's pleated shirt, a vicious red nail flicking at an onyx stud before she dropped her questing fingers farther, to his belly and then beyond.

"Why don't we find some place where we can be alone," she murmured, emphasizing the word "alone" with the firm pressure of her palm at the juncture of his thighs. She rubbed her sequined-clad body against his, thigh to thigh, breast to chest. "I know you want me and I want you, so let's forget the silly preliminaries and get to it."

Jordan wrapped his fingers around her bare shoulders and gently pushed her away from him. "Excuse me," he said, his voice cold and dispassionate. "There's someone I need to speak to. Here, drink this." He pushed a glass of champagne into Sirena Marsh's hand as he stepped away from her. "And try to relax," he added. "This is a party, after all."

Pete Stockton stood across the room, grinning from ear to ear, surrounded by three of Jordan's potential fiancées. He raised his glass to Jordan and Jordan nodded back grimly, inclining his head toward the kitchen door, a signal for Stockton to meet him there. Pete extracted himself from the group and made his way across the crowded living room to join Jordan.

"Four down, one to go," Jordan muttered as he pushed the swinging door open. Weaving through the chaotic mess in the kitchen, Jordan led Pete through the breakfast nook and out to the balcony. The icy air and pristine quiet were a soothing balm to his ragged nerves. He took a deep breath and let it out slowly, a cloud of vapor drifting into the night.

"Don't tell me. Let me guess," Pete said. "You don't like her."

"At least you're right about one thing. Where did you find these women?" Jordan asked, his jaw tight with tension. "First, she shoved me into a dark corner, then she practically emasculated me with those fingernails of hers. I have never met a more aggressive woman in my life. I have to tell you, Pete, that one actually scared me."

"So I missed the mark on Sirena Marsh. What about the others?"

"Lucy McMahon spent twenty-five minutes telling me about her last boyfriend. They broke up six months ago and she's carrying a torch the size of the Statue of Liberty's for the guy. I'm not going to marry a woman on the rebound."

"Yeah, she told me about Larry. I got the condensed version, though. What about Amanda Witherspoon? It looked like you were getting along fine with her. She's intelligent and a knockout."

"She's also engaged. She and Nick Trent's son just announced their engagement last weekend. He's just taken over his father's New York office. Unlike poor Lucy, Amanda is deliriously happy."

"All right, I'll admit my intelligence on Amanda was a little out of date. That leaves Lauren. She looked like a good candidate. I noticed she had a cold, so she probably wasn't at her best. What did you think?"

"Lauren has allergies. She spent our entire conversation blowing her nose and listing the multitude of substances that set off her sneezing and sniffles. My shampoo and my cologne appeared midway down the list. She also informed me that the carpeting was giving her hives and the smell of shellfish was making her nauseous." Jordan rubbed his forehead with his fingertips. "I think it would be best if I met number five and then called it a night."

"Ah, that's not going to be possible," Pete said, turning to gaze out at the lake. "She left."

"She left?"

"Well, actually, she was carried out. It seems Miss Caroline Simmons has a propensity to overindulge in champagne. It happened while you were occupied with Sirena. Count yourself lucky, though. Amanda told me the last party Caroline attended she finished the evening on top of the dining-room table singing her rendition of 'Some Enchanted Evening.' It was not a pretty sight."

"I thought I could trust you to take care of this matter," Jordan said.

"All these women looked great on paper. And I didn't have enough time to check them out personally."

Jordan tipped his head back and sighed, realizing that his assistant wasn't at fault. "Send them all home, Pete," he said, his voice betraying his weariness. "This party was a waste of time."

"Okay, boss. Whatever you say."

As Pete stepped through the sliding-glass doors, Jordan leaned to rest his elbows on the railing and looked out over the lake. On the horizon, the constellation Orion was barely visible through the spill of light from the city. Jordan stared at the hunter stars, finding Rigel and Betelgeuse, the brightest stars in the constellation and recalling his father's patient instructions in astronomy.

They had gazed at the stars on a night much like this nearly thirty years ago and they had talked of Jordan's dreams. "Someday I'll fly in a giant rocket to one of those stars," Jordan had promised, "and I'll steal one from the sky and bring it back to you in a jar." His father had laughed and ruffled his hair, then hoisted him up on his shoulder. "Show me which star you'll steal," his father had said, and Jordan had pointed to the heavens, picking out Rigel.

He remembered that night with such clarity; it was the first time he had seen his father smile in a very long time. It would also be the last, for the morning after that crystalline night, Jordan's mother walked out for good. At first, his father had tried to explain. He had been working too much, Jordan's mother was lonely; he wasn't able to give her what she wanted in a husband; she would be back soon. But then he had stopped trying to make excuses and lapsed into a long silence.

James Prentiss had become more and more preoccupied, spending his evenings alone, closeted in his study while his son waited outside. Most nights his father had never come out. Once, Jordan had sneaked in and found him sprawled on the couch, an empty crystal decanter in his hand.

There had been arguments between his grandfather and his father, the frequency increasing as his father's growing ineffectiveness as president of BabyLove began to show.

His father had succumbed to a heart attack when Jordan was sixteen. By that time, the company his grandfather had founded had floundered. The old man assumed the presidency, but he was unfamiliar with the changing market climate, with the baby boom and broadcast advertising, with supermarket-chain distribution and the competition from the major food conglomerates. Jonathan Prentiss kept the company running just long enough for Jordan to gain the skills and the experience needed to run BabyLove. Upon his grandfather's death four years ago, Jordan was handed the presidency of a company that was on the brink of failure.

No one had ever asked him whether he wanted it or not, it was just given to him as part of his legacy. The Prentiss legacy. And it was the only tool he had left to erase his mother's desertion and his father's mistakes. The company was his life. He knew every corner of the business. And he had been the one to snatch it from the jaws of death to make it what it was today.

He would do anything to preserve that legacy. Anything. He owed it to his father. The little boy who had dreamed of becoming an astronaut still lived inside him, but that boy had grown to be a man and had learned to appreciate what his grandfather and his father had built for him. He was not about to let it go. Not without a fight.

Jordan closed his eyes and let his tense neck muscles relax. When he had first decided on this plan, it seemed acceptable considering the alternatives. But now, the thought of marriage set his senses on edge. It should have been so simple, a business arrangement, a partnership between a man and a woman, with no expectations of love and no need for emotional surrender. She would offer him stability and he would offer her security. It would be a fair trade.

But now that plan no longer seemed workable. Why not? his thoughts demanded. Just what was it he was looking for? Could it be that he wanted more than a business arrangement? Jordan shook his head, trying to sort out the melee of contradictions that plagued his mind. One image, one name, surfaced over and over again, breaking through the muddle.

Elise. Elise Sinclair.

Dammit, why was she doing this to him? Until he had met Elise Sinclair, he had never considered romance a necessary part of a relationship. But she seemed to thrive on it, as if it were a necessary component of life, like breathing or eating or sleeping. Everything about her exuded romance, her soft, melodic voice, her graceful movements, her rose-colored view of the world.

A week ago, he would have written her off as some poor starry-eyed fool with nothing better to do than fantasize about love, an emotion that would never survive in the harsh, real world. But she had turned the tables on him. The fact that he appeared deficient in her eyes because of his lack of romantic skills bothered him. He always prided himself in being a highly educated man. Now he found his education sadly limited in the one area that counted to her—and to hundreds of other women, as well.

So what did he want? He wanted Elise Sinclair. But he needed a wife. And if he couldn't separate the two, then he was in worse shape than he'd imagined.

Jordan pushed himself away from the railing and stepped back into the kitchen. After adjusting to the cold on the balcony, he found the heat from his apartment smothering. The caterers rushed around the kitchen, clattering trays and clinking glasses, the noise grating against his nerves. Jordan peeked through the swinging door. The crowd had thinned considerably, enough for him to make it through the living room and to the door without much notice, he thought.

Jordan checked his pocket for his keys, then headed for the front door, grabbing his coat on the way and mumbling his goodbyes to the remaining guests. Five minutes later, he turned his Mercedes onto Lake Shore Drive and headed north, the sunroof open to the winter wind and the radio tuned to an all-night jazz station. He drove along the lake as far as Ravinia Park, then turned around and wove his way back through the city.

It was after midnight when he pulled up across the street from Elise's house. Jordan silenced the engine, but left the radio playing softly in the background.

At first he refused to look at the house, angry that he had been drawn to this place against his typically unyielding will. But slowly, he let his gaze drift along the sidewalk and up her front steps. The first and second floors were dark, but a light burned in the window of the third floor. Was she awake?

His imagination slowly played with the possibilities. He would walk to the front door and ring the bell. She would answer and he would pull her into his arms and kiss her. She would be surprised, but she would return his kiss, opening herself to him. He would lead her to the bedroom, undressing her along the way. And then they would make love.

His fantasy came to a grinding halt. Make love? No, they wouldn't *make love;* they would have sex. He had never made love to a woman in his life. Love had nothing to do with the physical release he felt with a woman.

But that wasn't what he wanted to feel when he imagined moving inside of Elise. He wanted a deeper connection; he wanted to surrender himself, to take shelter in her warmth. Suddenly, he wanted to feel more than just the release, he longed to appreciate the significance of the act, to strip away the physical pleasure until all that was left was the pure emotion behind that pleasure.

A shadow suddenly appeared at the window and he instinctively slouched in his seat, trying not to be seen in the feeble glow of the streetlight above his car. He held his breath, then slowly released it when he saw that it wasn't her. The outline of a cat became clear against the light that filtered through the lace curtain. The cat seemed to be looking directly at him.

Jordan straightened in his seat. With his eyes still fixed on the window, he turned the key in the ignition, then pulled the car away from the curb. He dragged his gaze from the house at the last minute.

Thank God it had only been a cat at the window, Jordan thought, because if it had been Elise, he wasn't sure if he could have stopped himself from going inside.

ON TUESDAY MORNING, Elise stood in the center of the Gold Coast Room, her gaze gliding up the huge columns to the ornate gilt plaster ceiling and sparkling chandeliers above. The woman from the Drake's catering staff had left her alone to await Jordan's arrival, rushing off to handle an emergency. Elise was glad to have a moment of solitude. Though Jordan wasn't due for another fifteen minutes, she could sense her rising anticipation.

With a frustrated sigh, she tried to put his image out of her mind for what seemed like the millionth time that day. Instead she closed her eyes and imagined the room as it would look for the Prentiss wedding.

The room would be flooded with midmorning light from the huge windows that overlooked the Oak Street Beach. The rough wooden tables that cluttered the room would be covered with crisp white linen and table runners of white brocade edged in gold, then topped with gleaming silver, china and crystal. She would crown each table with a towering vase of calla lilies and blush roses interlaced with tropical greenery. Uniformed waiters would serve a luscious brunch of lobster medallions on a puff pastry with a light hollandaise sauce. And during brunch, a small orchestra would play soft, romantic music.

She could almost hear the music, the lyric strains of a Gershwin ballad. She hummed a few bars, swaying to the tune, the words passing her lips in a soft song. With a sigh, she moved to the piano at the edge of the dance floor and slid onto the bench. The tune meandered through her mind and she searched for the notes on the keyboard.

Ten years of childhood piano lessons and hours of painstaking practice had paid off. She added the harmony line to Gershwin's "Isn't It Romantic?" and lost herself in the music, embellishing the tune more with each repetition. At first, she hummed along with the piano, then quietly sang the words, slightly off-key. As the music progressed, Elise sang a little louder, her wavering voice cutting though the silence of the ballroom.

She closed her eyes as she played and sang, an image of Jordan appearing in her mind. He was dressed in the formal attire of a morning wedding: gray cutaway coat, striped trousers and paisley ascot. His dark hair fell across his forehead and his mouth was turned up in a warm smile. His bride stood beside him, resplendent in a dress of ivory silk organza and Alençon lace. Out of the haze of her daydream, the bride's features materialized and Elise found herself staring at her own image. She forced her eyes open, shocked by the direction of her dreams.

But her innocent dreams were much less disturbing than the reality of Jordan's presence. He stood beside the piano watching her, one eyebrow raised questioningly.

Elise jumped up from her seat with a startled yelp. The piano bench tipped over behind her with a loud thud. Catching her balance, she grabbed for the music rack, only to send the cover crashing down over the keys. She stepped out from behind the keyboard and nervously smoothed her skirt.

"I didn't hear you come in," she said, an accusing note in her voice.

"I know," he replied. He took a step closer. "You play very well."

Elise smiled tremulously. "Thank you." She took a deep breath and met his blue eyes squarely. "Aren't you going to compliment my singing?"

His expression became serious. "Ah, that's what that was. Singing. A very interesting approach, though I hope you don't have your heart set on a career in opera."

Elise caught the glint of humor in his eyes and laughter bubbled from her throat. "If you were truly a gentleman, you would have complimented my singing, as well. It would have been the polite thing to do."

"I prefer honesty over the conventions of etiquette. And I was being honest about your playing. You are quite good."

"Then I accept your compliment, on behalf of myself, my mother and Mrs. Merriweather."

"Mrs. Merriweather?"

"My piano teacher. She lived down the street from us and I used to go to her house every Tuesday after school. When I played well, she put a gold star at the top of the page. And when I played poorly, she would upbraid me thoroughly and send me straight home. I'm lucky I never sang for her. I'm sure she would have either scolded me senseless or moved out of the neighborhood, never to be seen again."

Jordan's expression softened and his smile lit up his eyes. "My childhood nemesis was Miss Winifred Ivey. She was a tyrant in tap shoes and she ran a dancing school. On Saturday mornings, she would hold me and nineteen other boys and girls hostage, teaching us the social graces and the box step."

He stepped in front of her, placing one arm behind his back and one over his stomach, bowing stiffly from the waist. "May I have the pleasure of this dance, Miss Sinclair?" He held out his hand and she placed her fingers in his, her laughter echoing through the ballroom.

Suddenly the cool, reserved man had disappeared and Elise found herself looking at a different Jordan— smiling, teasing, at ease. The tension she usually felt when she was with him dissolved and she returned his relaxed humor. "I would be delighted, Mr. Prentiss." He took her to the middle of the dance floor and led her though a clumsy version of the box step, holding her at arm's length. For a short time, she thought he was being deliberately uncoordinated, treading on her toes on purpose. But when she looked up at the determined expression on his face, she realized that he really couldn't dance.

"You're almost as bad a dancer as I am a singer."

"Miss Ivey's Saturday-morning assemblies were not my idea of fun. I did my best to forget everything she taught me."

"Don't you get to practice at all those society functions you're always attending? I read about the Lyric Opera Ball and it sounded so romantic, a masque ball with Viennese waltzing and champagne. You must have danced at least once with Danielle Langley."

Jordan glanced down at her with a puzzled expression. "Who?"

"Danielle Langley." His expression remained the same. "Your date," she explained.

"She was my date?"

"Yes," Elise cried. "I saw a picture of you both in an old issue of *Town and Country*."

Jordan shrugged. "I don't remember."

"You've dated a lot of women, haven't you?"

"You seem to know more about the details of my social life than I do. *You* tell *me*. Have I dated a lot of women, Miss Sinclair?" His gaze met hers.

She looked away and studied her fingers spread across his upper arm. "Yes, you have."

"Is there anything wrong with that?"

"No. In fact, it's probably good. You were sowing your wild oats."

"I was what?"

"You know, playing the field. Getting it out of your system."

"'It?'"

Elise looked up at him and saw the laughter in his eyes. She smiled. "You're teasing me. And you're also not concentrating on your dancing. You really should try to learn."

"Since dancing is not a prerequisite for business success, I guess I'll survive."

"But what about your wedding? You'll have to dance with your bride. It's tradition. The first dance is the highlight of the reception. Maybe you could take dancing lessons. Just a few until you feel comfortable."

"Or maybe we could waive the tradition."

"Oh, no," Elise cried, stopping suddenly. "You can't do that. Your bride would be so disappointed and so would your guests. And it is such a romantic part of the whole wedding. I just love to watch the first dance. It always brings tears to my eyes."

"Then teach me," Jordan said in a warm tone. "Right here, right now."

Elise looked up at him, trying to hide her sudden discomfort. She felt herself grow tense as she realized the impact their innocent dance was having on her senses. Being in the same room with Jordan Prentiss was hard enough, but being in his arms one moment longer would be unbearable—and highly improper. Dancing lessons were certainly beyond her duties as a wedding consultant. "There's no music. I can't teach you to dance without music."

"What was that song you were singing when I came in? Sing that."

Elise shook her head and tried to pull away from him, but he held fast.

"Teach me," he urged. "I need to know these things."

He began to hum the tune, faltering slightly at first until she hummed along with him. She paused in her humming to offer him instruction. "First, you need to relax. Don't hold your arms so stiff." He loosened his grip on her and let his arms relax, but instead of gaining distance, she found herself slipping closer to his body.

"Now, start moving like this, back and forth with the music." He followed her swaying footsteps. When he had mastered the basics, she moved him in a slow circle on the dance floor. "When you dance with your bride, you will lead her, and she will follow your lead."

"Why?" Jordan asked, staring at his feet. "I'm the one who doesn't know how to dance."

"That's the way it's done. Don't you remember anything Miss Ivey taught you? Now you try. You lead me where you want to go." He slowly drew her in a circle around the dance floor and she smiled. He was a quick student. Already his movements were becoming smooth and more natural. "Don't watch your feet. Look into your bride's eyes when you dance with her. Show her that she's the most beautiful woman in the world to you."

Jordan lifted his chin and his gaze locked with hers. She stumbled slightly. Her mind raced as they stared at each other, her thoughts a jumble of confusion. For an instant she thought she saw desire in the depths of his pale eyes, and a wave of apprehension rippled through her body. What was he doing? What did he want? Her heart hammered in her chest and her breath caught in her throat. Slowly he drew her nearer, still moving to the silent music that passed between them, tipping his head as if to prepare to kiss her.

Elise tore herself from the circle of his arms and turned her back on him. With her knees shaking and her nerves humming, she walked to the relative safety of the piano. "I think you have the idea. Maybe you should practice with your fiancée."

"Maybe," she heard Jordan say in a soft voice.

Elise turned to face him. The mask of reserve again covered his expression.

Lord, her imagination was running away with her! That hadn't been desire in his eyes. He was an engaged man, in love with his bride-to-be. And she was a lovesick fool, transforming his every word and action into some gesture of reciprocal feeling.

"Why don't we discuss the wedding plans?" Elise said, moving to the table near the dance floor that held her briefcase. "Let me tell you about the menu first." Elise efficiently recited her recommendations, keeping her eyes focused on her notes and glancing up only briefly to catch Jordan's replies to her questions. When she finished reviewing the menu, she described the decor she had planned for the ballroom. As her presentation progressed she found herself getting caught up in the excitement of the wedding plans. She pushed her feelings for Jordan to the back of her mind and let her professional expertise take over.

"I think your wedding will be the most romantic affair Chicago has ever seen," Elise concluded, her voice filled with pride. She put her papers in her briefcase and snapped the lid shut.

Jordan regarded her with a serious look. "Romantic. You use that word a lot."

"Do I?" She shrugged. "I never noticed."

"It's important to you . . . this romance?"

"Of course. Not just to me, but to all women. Romance makes love exciting. That's what I enjoy about planning weddings—adding romance to people's lives, making their weddings like a dream come true."

"I'm not a very romantic person," Jordan admitted in a sober voice. "At least, that's what I've been told."

Elise hid her amusement at his confession. "I sensed that about you," she replied. "From the moment we met, I wondered how you ever got your fiancée to agree to marry you."

"You make marriage to me sound like a prison sentence. I'm not such a bad guy."

"I'm sure you're not. You're practical and honest. But terribly preoccupied and definitely not a romantic."

"You know a lot about romance, don't you? You're something of an expert in the field."

"I know how I like to be treated. I guess I feel pretty much like other women do. I like to be courted, to feel special, like the most desirable woman in the world."

Jordan paused for a moment before replying. "And how would a man go about doing that?"

Elise looked at him incredulously. "You're asking me?"

"Yes. Tell me what to do. Tell me how to be more romantic."

Elise considered his request for a moment. Teaching him to dance had gotten her in enough trouble. What would advising him in the art of romance lead to? She made her decision in a split second—she would have to refuse. This was not part of her professional responsibilities.

But, then, she was in the business of planning the perfect wedding. And the perfect wedding required a perfect bridegroom, a wonderfully romantic bridegroom. Maybe it wouldn't hurt to give Jordan a few pointers.

"All right. Tell me your idea of a romantic evening."

Jordan's brow furrowed as he considered her request. "Dinner at a nice restaurant?" he began, seeking her approval immediately.

"That's a start."

"Flowers."

"What kind?"

"Roses." He looked at her again for an indication of her assent, but she made no move to agree with his choice.

"And champagne," he continued. "Champagne is very romantic, isn't it?"

"It can be." She was silent, waiting for him to go on. "Is that all?"

"Isn't that enough?"

Elise shook her head. "That's all so ordinary. Real romance comes from the unexpected. Dinner at a hotdog stand, a bouquet of dandelions and a bottle of root beer can be much more romantic than what you described. Remember, you want her to feel special. Be spontaneous. Now, what would you consider a romantic gift?"

Jordan regarded her warily before he answered. "Diamonds."

"No, no, no. Diamonds are ordinary. They're boring. Think of something special. It doesn't have to be expensive."

"Rubies? Wait, no, that's not the right answer," Jordan said. "Hell, I hate tests. Garnets. That's what I meant to say."

Elise groaned in dismay. "Generic jewels are about the most unromantic gift a woman could receive. I'd much rather get a unique pair of inexpensive earrings—earrings that a man picked out because they reminded him of me—than all the diamonds in the world."

"I don't believe you," Jordan scoffed. "All women love diamonds."

"I know it sounds trite, but it *is* the thought that counts. It doesn't matter how much a gift costs. If it's a gift from the heart, its value is priceless. Do you understand?"

Jordan shot her a skeptical look. "No, I don't. What woman in her right mind would want cheap earrings instead of a diamond necklace? That's just idiotic . . . it's baffling . . ." He sighed. "And it's just like a woman."

Elise grinned. "You're learning." She stood up, pulled on her coat and grabbed her briefcase. "Come on. We're finished here. There's a flower shop off the lobby. Let's go down there and you can pick out something for . . ." Elise paused. "You could at least tell me her first name. I'm getting tired of calling her 'your fiancée' or 'your bride.' What should I call her?"

Jordan hesitated before he spoke. Surely he hadn't forgotten her name! Or maybe he was just trying to decide whether he could trust her. He regarded her with a suspicious look before he finally spit out a name.

"Abby. My fiancée's name is Abby."

A sudden surge of guilt coursed through Elise's body. Abby. Before she had been a nameless, faceless woman, someone who didn't exist in Elise's mind. Now she had suddenly become real, and Elise felt a rush of self-recrimination flood her soul.

He was an engaged man, she told herself again, the meaning finally hitting home. Somewhere on the planet was a woman named Abby who would stand beside him at the altar, make love to him in his bed and bear his children. Somewhere there was an Abby who loved Jordan Prentiss. And here she stood, Elise Sinclair, ridiculously enamored with Abby's fiancé.

Elise forced a smile to her lips. "Abby," she repeated. "Let's go find a romantic bouquet of flowers for Abby."

She walked through the ballroom, her steps brisk and businesslike, and descended the stairs with Jordan at her side.

The flower shop was unoccupied except for the young woman who stood behind the counter. The woman eyed Jordan appreciatively as he stood before her, and Elise stifled an unwelcome twinge of jealousy.

"We'd like to put together a bouquet of flowers," Elise said, trying unsuccessfully to draw the girl's attention.

"Romantic flowers," Jordan added with a crooked smile.

"All our flowers are romantic," the salesgirl answered flirtatiously. "What would you like? How about some long-stemmed roses?"

Jordan turned to Elise and leaned closer. "I guess she isn't a graduate of the Sinclair School of Romance, huh?" he whispered, his breath tickling her ear.

She ignored the shiver that ran through her and silently repeated the name "Abby" again and again, an incantation against her perfidious feelings.

Elise looked over the girl's shoulder to the refrigerated case behind her. "Let's start with a dozen of those daffodils." The girl retrieved the daffodils and placed them on a wide piece of paper on the counter. "Then let's add some of the freesia."

Elise picked up a stalk of the freesia and held it under Jordan's nose. "Here, smell *this*," she ordered.

He breathed in the scent and a smile lit his face. "Lemons. It smells like lemons."

Elise took the freesia and placed it under her nose, brushing the soft petals beneath her chin and inhaling the fresh scent of springtime. "It almost makes you forget it's winter, doesn't it?" Elise turned back to the salesgirl. "Add a few of those daisies, too. Then wrap them up."

When the flowers were securely wrapped against the cold outdoors, she handed the bundle to Jordan. "Next time, try this on your own. Avoid the roses and choose something that reminds you of her. It will be much more thoughtful that way."

As they walked through the lobby and out the front doors onto Walton Place, Elise was smiling. She had helped Jordan, in a small way, to understand what would make Abby happy. Somehow the gesture made up for her traitorous behavior.

"I'll call you in a few days," Elise said in a business-like tone. "We'll need to get you, your best man and your ushers in for a fitting for your cutaways. You'll need at least four ushers, preferably six, considering the size of your guest list. I'll also put together a checklist of things you'll need to take care of and another list for you to discuss with your fian—Abby."

"Can I give you a ride home?" Jordan asked.

"No, I have a couple of more errands to run and I have an appointment uptown for lunch. I'll talk to you soon." Elise stepped into a waiting cab, closing the door behind her. She waved to Jordan through the window, then fixed her gaze on the street in front of her.

An odd feeling of loneliness descended on her as the cab sped away, and she was tempted to look back, to look at Jordan one more time. But she resisted the temptation. It was best to put as much distance between them as possible, both physical and mental. And

the best way to accomplish that would be to put Abby
directly in between them.

Abby was the key to eliminating her attraction to
Jordan. Elise made a silent vow to force the issue of
Abby's absence at the next available opportunity. If she
didn't, she could not continue working with Jordan. For
she knew, deep in her heart, that she would never find
Jordan anything but an endlessly fascinating, hope-
lessly unattainable man.

JORDAN WATCHED Elise's cab disappear around the corner onto Michigan Avenue, then looked up and down
the street for his driver. The limo was parked halfway
down the block. Before his driver could catch sight of
him, Jordan turned and walked in the opposite direction, avoiding a return to the office.

Oak Street Beach was deserted except for a few
hearty joggers who passed him on the wide walkway.
The strident noise of the city traffic blended with the
soothing sound of the waves rushing against the dunes
of ice that covered the beach. Jordan pulled the collar
of his coat up and hunched his shoulders against the
numbing wind coming off the lake. He breathed deeply
of the frigid air, and it rejuvenated him physically, but
his thoughts were still centered on his disturbing encounter with Elise Sinclair.

Though he had tried to deny his feelings at every
turn, Elise was becoming a constant presence in his
thoughts. They were polar opposites, yet his attraction to her was magnetic, dangerously overpowering
but completely irresistible. She was everything he had
set his mind against, but still he wanted her with a thirst
that couldn't be quenched and a hunger that refused to
be sated. He knew she had captured his mind the mo-

ment they met and now his body had begun to betray
him, too.

He could still feel the warmth of her long, slender
fingers wrapped in his, could still smell the fresh floral
scent of her hair. He ripped open the package of flowers and withdrew a stalk of freesia. Touching the soft
flowers to his lips as she had, he inhaled their scent.
When they had danced, it had been nearly impossible
to keep himself from pulling her firmly into his arms
and taking what he wanted. He knew instinctively how
her sweet, soft lips would taste to his tongue, how her
warm, pliant body would respond to his hands.

Jordan sat down on a low stone bench and stared
abstractedly at a small flock of pigeons that had gathered at his feet. He wanted Elise and he needed a wife.
So why couldn't they be one and the same? She fit all
the basic requirements and she possessed an added at-
tribute—she was sexually attractive to him. Maybe he
could combine the best of both worlds. Elise could
make a perfect wife and a perfect lover.

Yes, Elise would meet all his requirements, but could
he meet all hers? He had known her only a week, but
he knew precisely what she wanted from a husband.
She wanted love. Not just ordinary everyday love, but
unconditional, undying, twenty-four-hour-a-day love.
Love served up with a healthy dose of romance. She
wanted the hearts and the flowers and the violins playing in the background.

She wanted exactly what he could never give her.

He had never been in love in his life and considered
the prospect of falling in love a remote possibility at
best. Love was an emotion that was entirely unfathomable to him. It defied logic and reason, it was unpredictable. Worst of all, love was something he could

not control, and Jordan did not allow anything into his
life that he could not control.

So what were his options? Jordan ticked them off in
his mind, considering each and drawing a conclusion
regarding its chances of success before moving on, an
approach he used every day making business decisions
at BabyLove.

Option one: he could tell Elise he loved her. It would
be a lie, but it seemed like the simplest way to get everything he wanted. But the thought of deceiving Elise
was shockingly distasteful. Lying to her about his fiancée's name had been deceitful. Lying to her about love
would be criminal.

Option two: he could tell Elise the truth about his
immediate need for a wife and hope she might accept a
business partnership over a loving marriage. There
wasn't much possibility of her going for that considering her starry-eyed vision of love.

Or he could go on with his plans to find a bride and
try to seduce Elise, as well. Chances for success? Less
than zero.

Or he could just forget Elise altogether.

All things considered, the last option seemed the
most likely. Elise was a complication he did not need,
an inconvenient detour on the direct route to his most
important goal—saving his company.

So he would put her out of his mind, he determined.
But not completely. She did have one thing he couldn't
do without. Her romantic advice could prove to be
quite useful in his search for a bride. Time was running
out and anything that could secure the future of Baby-
Love was definitely worth trying.

Jordan stood up, scattering the pigeons, and walked
back toward Michigan Avenue. In a heedless motion,

he tossed the bundle of flowers into a trash can along the way. He took several steps, then stopped and returned to the trash can to retrieve a stalk of freesia.

With gentle fingers, he tucked the scented flowers inside his coat and turned away, a smile curving his lips. Then he picked up his pace, anxious to return to the office and resume his search for a bride. With an organized approach, and a little romance thrown in, he was sure he would have a fiancée within the next month. After all, how hard could it possibly be to learn what really pleased a woman? He just needed a few pointers and a little practice. And what better way to start than with a simple gesture of appreciation in return for Elise's help?

The only immediate problem was where to find dandelions in the dead of winter.

4

"NOW I KNOW why we don't let the grooms plan the weddings," Elise railed as she slammed the phone into the cradle. "It must have something to do with a missing chromosome in the male of the species. They have no comprehension of the importance of the event, no understanding of the necessity for schedules." Her voice rose in volume, taking on a slightly hysterical note. "If we left weddings to the men, no one would ever get married. Society as we know it would cease to exist. The entire human race would slowly disappear. We'd all be doomed." She paused in her tirade for a moment before continuing in a shriek, "I thought I told you to get off the counter!"

Clorinda glanced up at her, taking a short respite from licking out an empty frosting bowl to shoot Elise a malevolent look. Elise stepped toward her, wielding a wooden spoon with enough menace to make the feline think twice about remaining in the room. In a flurry of fur, the cat jumped from the counter and raced out of the kitchen. Thisbe trotted out after her.

"Not so loud," Dona said calmly, her concentration centered on the sugar-paste lily she was sculpting. "These flowers take a steady hand." When she finished the flower, she carefully transferred it to the top of one of Elise's tiny engagement cakes, then let out her pent-up breath. "There. Perfect." She turned to Elise. "Now, what has you so upset?"

"Jordan Prentiss, that's what . . . or who! And his mysterious bride, Abby. She cares even less about this wedding than he does, if that's possible. I just called him to give him the name of the formal-wear shop where he and his wedding attendants need to go for their fittings. Then I naively asked him to find out where his bride bought her wedding gown. I'm in charge of selecting the maid of honor's dress, so I wanted to find something that complemented the bridal gown. Do you know what he told me?"

Dona shook her head, her attention now focused on placing the finished cake in a small foil box.

"He told me she hadn't selected her gown yet. The wedding is less than three months away and she doesn't have a wedding gown. And then to top it all off, he told me I should choose the bridal gown along with the honor attendant's dress."

"That sounds nice," Dona replied.

Elise could tell her best friend wasn't paying a bit of attention to her dilemma. Whenever Dona was in the same room with a bowl of cake batter, all else took a back seat to her art, including Elise. In fact, she sometimes believed that her friend had batter running through her veins and butter-cream frosting for brains.

Dona pushed the box across the counter. "Isn't that pretty? This is sure to get you some new clients. Tell me, what woman could resist a precious little lily cake like that?"

Elise sat down on a kitchen stool, cupped her chin in her palm and picked up a frosting-coated knife. "It'd better work," she mumbled as she licked at the creamy icing. "After what I just said to Jordan Prentiss, he may be looking for a new wedding consultant."

"What are you talking about?"

"I told him it was against my policy to choose the wedding gown for the bride. I told him this was not the proper time to be speaking for his bride and that he should tell Abby she must choose her own dress."

"And what did he say?"

"Nothing at first. Then he said, fine, he would pass along my advice and that I should choose a variety of appropriate gowns and have them delivered to his office to be shown to her privately."

"So, what's the problem?"

"Don't you find it a bit strange that the bride hasn't shown one ounce of interest in the most important day of her life? And isn't it odd that I haven't been allowed to meet the bride? Why is her identity such a big secret? I had to practically twist Prentiss's arm before he would even tell me her first name. And I know he makes all the decisions on his own, without even consulting her. This whole wedding is positively weird."

"I've heard that the rich and powerful can be a little eccentric. As long as he's paying you, I wouldn't worry too much. And is it absolutely necessary for you to meet the bride?"

"No, not absolutely," Elise replied, her mouth pursed in an indignant pout. She grabbed a rolling pin and attacked a ball of fondant, rolling the doughlike frosting out to the proper thickness. As Elise worked, her pout slowly transformed to a sly smile. "But, I have a plan," she continued, "that might just flush the future Mrs. Prentiss out into the open. And I have a feeling once she gets a taste of wedding magic, she'll jump right into the excitement, head-first."

Dona took the sheet of fondant and covered a tiny cake, sealing the edges to keep it fresh and provide an even surface for her frosting art. "How are you going to accomplish that?"

"I'll set up an after-hours appointment for her at The Ideal Bride. Sheila will be happy to keep the shop open for a commission like the one she'll get on this dress. Then I'll be there to help in the selection. I'll take the opportunity to discuss the wedding plans with the mysterious Abby and figure out why Prentiss is so protective of his fiancée."

"Sounds like a good plan to me. Now, on to more important matters—what do you have planned for my pretty little cakes?"

The doorbell sounded from the front of the house. Elise jumped up and dusted off her hands on her striped apron. "Melvin, the owner of Lakeshore Florists, is sending over one of his delivery boys to pick them up later this afternoon," she said. "I promised him the florals on the Prentiss wedding plus any of the weddings we get from this promotion in trade for delivering fifty cakes."

Elise hurried to the foyer and swung the front door open. A young man stood on her stoop, his cold-reddened fingers clutching a small white box. At first, Elise thought he was from Melvin's, but then she noticed the name of another florist embroidered on his jacket.

"I have a delivery for Miss Elise Sinclair," he said.

"I'm Elise Sinclair."

He thrust a clipboard at her and she signed for the flowers.

Elise walked back to the kitchen with the box, her curiosity piqued. Who would be sending her flowers? It wasn't her birthday and there wasn't a man in her life. That eliminated both causes for a gift of flowers. And the box was not the typical elongated package that usually carried long-stemmed roses. There was no cellophane window to allow a glimpse into the contents and no card to give a clue to the sender's identity. She pushed open the swinging door to the kitchen.

"Who was at the door?" Dona asked, her attention now focused on coloring a bowl of sugar paste the proper shade of green.

"A delivery boy from Colin's Florals. He brought me some flowers."

"Who would be sending you flowers?" Dona's attention wandered for a moment in Elise's direction. "You haven't been holding out on me, have you? Are you dating someone I don't know about?"

"No," she answered, continuing to stare at the box. "You know how long it's been since my last date. You remind me of it at least once a week."

Dona dropped what she was doing and walked over to examine the box closely. "Well, why don't you open it? Maybe you have a secret admirer."

Elise slid her finger under the flap and popped open the top. Wading through layers of tissue paper, she finally came upon a tiny bouquet, festooned with ribbons and lace, nestled in the bottom of the box.

A tiny bouquet of dandelions.

"A very sick secret admirer," Dona commented as she grabbed the box. "Is this some kind of joke? Who would send you dandelions? They're weeds."

"No, they're not," Elise cried defensively, snatching the box back. She pulled the wilted bouquet from the tissue paper. "They're very...romantic." The greenery surrounding the yellow flowers looked fresh and alive, but the dandelions had seen better days. She brought the bouquet to her nose and instinctively inhaled deeply. An irritating smell tickled her nose and made her eyes water. She sneezed, once...twice...three times, before she dropped the bouquet back into the box.

"Very romantic," Dona repeated, her voice dripping with sarcasm. "The guy who sent them must be a real catch."

Elise reluctantly closed the box, pushing it away from her. "He is . . . or will be after I get done with him."

"Then you know who sent these?"

"Yes."

Dona watched her, waiting for her to continue. Elise knew her friend wouldn't let the subject drop so easily. They had no secrets between them when it came to men—except for one now.

"I'm waiting," Dona said.

"All right. I know who sent them." Elise sighed. "Jordan Prentiss."

"The man with the missing chromosome? The man you called a loathsome Lothario? The Caveman Bridegroom? I thought you were exaggerating. I didn't think any man could be that bad, but I guess you were right."

"He isn't that bad. He just doesn't understand women. I gave him a few pointers about romance and he took them a bit too literally."

"He sent you dandelions, Elise. I think you need to send him back to Remedial Romance 101."

"Jordan can be very romantic. When we were dancing at the—"

"You went dancing with Jordan?" Dona eyed Elise suspiciously. "And when did he go from 'Prentiss the Pain' to 'Jordan the Romantic?' And why is he sending you flowers? What's going on between the two of you?"

"Nothing! It's not what you think." Elise felt her face color. "The flowers are simply a thank-you for my help. If there were really something romantic between us, don't you think he would have sent roses? You're letting your imagination run away with you."

"Am I imagining that blush on your face? Come on, Elise, tell the truth. Are you and Jordan Prentiss having an affair?"

"No!"

"Are you in love with him?"

"No." Elise heard the lack of conviction in her voice. "Not exactly."

"What does that mean?"

"I just have—I just *had* a little crush on him, that's all. It was nothing, just a silly infatuation."

"He's engaged, Elise."

"I know that. That's why it's over. It was entirely harmless. But he's a very compelling man. Any warm-blooded woman would find him attractive, including you. So don't get worked up into one of your mother-hen snits."

Dona shot her a long-suffering look. "I won't. Just as long as you don't let yourself get carried away in one of your romantic fantasies."

"It's a deal." Elise relaxed, hoping the subject was closed. "Now, let's finish up these cakes. The delivery boy will be here in a few hours."

Elise set to work encasing another cake in fondant, but her thoughts were drawn to the dandelion bouquet that lay wilting in its tissue-paper bed. Dandelions in the middle of winter. Where had he gotten them? He had probably paid a tidy sum to have some bemused florist pick them and ship them north to another florist who had the onerous task of fashioning the weeds into a bouquet. What had at first seemed like a simple gift suddenly took on complex proportions. Were they really just a gesture of appreciation, as she had told Dona? Or were they more?

As hard as she tried to deny it, an odd feeling of apprehension gnawed at her mind. Could Jordan Prentiss possibly have another motive for sending the bouquet?

THE SHOWROOM of The Ideal Bride was shrouded in shadows when Elise arrived. Sheila led her through the dimly lit salon, past mannequins dressed in their white wedding finery and past long racks of wedding gowns. They headed toward the spacious fitting rooms that lined the rear of the store.

"Is she here yet?" Elise whispered.

"No," Sheila replied in an equally quiet voice. "But he is."

"'He?'"

"Yes, the bridegroom. Your Mr. Smith. He arrived ten minutes ago. He's waiting in the Bourbonnais Room."

"Alone?"

"Yes. He said his fiancée had an unexpected schedule conflict. I told him she could have called to cancel the appointment, but he said something about wanting to get this over with as soon as possible. What does that mean?"

Elise strode toward the illuminated fitting room, her irritation rising. "I don't know, but I'm about to find out."

"You know your way around," Sheila called after her. "I'll be in the office if you need any help."

Elise stepped into the mirror-lined fitting room to find Jordan lounging on an upholstered settee, his briefcase open and a file folder spread across his lap. He looked up at her and smiled and her irritation rose another degree. Even more annoying was the skip in her heartbeat as she met his gaze.

"You're late," he commented. "I thought the appointment was for seven-thirty."

Elise returned his smile stiffly, gathering her resolve and refusing to give in to the overwhelming attraction she felt for the man. "I got caught in traffic and yes, the appointment was for seven-thirty—with Abby, not you. Where is she?"

"She had an—"

"Unexpected schedule conflict?" Elise finished, unable to hide the skepticism in her voice.

"Yes," Jordan said. "She asked that I convey her apologies and requested that we go ahead and choose a gown for her."

"No," Elise snapped. "I will not choose her wedding gown. We'll just have to reschedule the appointment."

"That won't be possible," Jordan replied, his voice even. "She's...left the country...on business. She won't be back . . . until just before the wedding."

Elise sensed an undercurrent of tension in his words and her anger died. He, too, seemed irritated by his bride's absence, his bluntly spoken words holding a hint of suppressed aggravation.

"She's very devoted to her career," he explained coolly. "An attitude I wholeheartedly support. Her business comes first. And since plans for the wedding can be completed without her, she didn't find it necessary to cancel her trip. I'm sorry if that inconveniences you in any way, but that's the way it has to be."

Elise studied his expression, trying to detect another clue to his feelings. But it was as if his features were carved from granite, hard and unyielding. She slowly shook her head and her shoulders slumped in resignation. "All right, you win. But if Abby can't be here to pick out her dress, then you'll have to."

"I know nothing about wedding dresses," Jordan countered. "That's what I hired you for."

"You may not know much now, but you will by the end of the evening," Elise assured him. "Come on, let's get started." She walked out the fitting-room door and into the showroom, then waited for him to join her. When he did, she casually strolled along the racks of dresses, pulling several out and examining them.

"First, I'll need you to describe Abby's figure type."

"Her what?" Jordan asked. His voice sounded oddly panicked.

"Her figure, the shape of her body. How tall is she? What size dress does she wear? Is she slender or more voluptuous? What color hair does she have? Does she have fair skin or is her skin olive toned?"

Jordan stared at the wedding dress Elise was holding. "You need to know all that just to pick out a wedding dress? Why can't we just take this one and be done with it? It's white and it has lots of that frilly stuff on it. I like it."

"This is a one-of-a-kind dress designed by Daniel Evans and this frilly stuff is Schiffli lace." She sighed. "We have to choose something that will look stunning on Abby. Now, tell me, how tall is she?"

"I don't know her exact height," Jordan answered.

Elise tried valiantly to control her frustration. How could such a brilliant businessman be so incredibly obtuse when it came to women? "Compared to me, is she taller or shorter?"

Jordan stepped toward her. He clasped his hands around her upper arms and pulled her close, the frothy skirt of the wedding dress the only barrier between their bodies. She could feel his warm breath against her forehead, his beard-roughened chin bumping against her nose. He pushed her back.

"She's about the same height as you are."

Elise tried to calm her pounding pulse, a rhythm set in motion by the touch of his warm fingers. "I'm five foot six," she said. "About how much does she weigh?"

She jumped slightly when she felt the touch of his hands on her waist and hips.

"Her figure is a lot like yours," he said, his voice deep and rough. "She has curves in all the right places, but she's not overweight. She's just right. What size are you?"

"I'm a size ten."

"I'm pretty sure that's her size, too," he said, his hands still resting on her waist.

Elise kept her gaze fixed on his chest, unwilling to allow herself to give in to the intense pleasure that his touch aroused. She cleared her throat. "And her hair color?"

Jordan moved his hand to touch her hair, pulling a strand from behind her ear and letting it slip through his fingers. "Spun gold," he murmured, "Touched with copper." She felt his fingers brush her cheek. "And her skin is like fine Chinese porcelain with a tint of pink. Very smooth. Very soft."

Elise pulled away from him and turned to replace the dress in the rack. Suddenly, as if his words had pulled a plug, she felt her self-esteem drain from her body. His glowing description of Abby made her feel like an ugly duckling being compared with a beautiful swan. No wonder Jordan was in love with his fiancée. Abby was curvaceous; Elise was slightly pudgy. Her skin was luminous, while Elise's was merely pale. And her hair shimmered like gold; Elise's was simply strawberry blond.

"She sounds like a very beautiful woman," Elise said, her back still to him.

"She is," Jordan answered. His voice sounded choked.

Elise turned and caught a fleeting look of discomfort cross his face. For a brief moment, she saw passion cloud his eyes before it evaporated behind his clear, blue gaze. She swallowed, the bitter taste of envy burning its way down her throat. How lucky Abby was to have a man like Jordan, a man who raved about her beauty as he had. Somehow she hadn't expected Jordan to be able to paint such a stunning picture of his fiancée. But his eloquent words were vivid proof of his love for Abby.

"With paler skin, I'd recommend a gown in ivory. Pure white would make Abby look a little washed out." She walked down the rack, pulling a variety of dresses out and handing them to Jordan. At the last moment, she chose her favorite gown, the gown she gazed at longingly every time she entered The Ideal Bride, the gown she would choose for her own wedding. When his arms were full, she grabbed several more dresses, then headed for the fitting room.

She quickly hung the dresses she carried on an extended hook, then took the gowns from Jordan's arms and hung them up, also. "This is a lovely gown," she said, pulling the first dress from the hook and holding it out to him. "It has simple lines that give it a medieval quality. And this is Chantilly lace," she explained, fingering the fine florals and scrolls embroidered on net. "It has gigot sleeves and a bateau neckline."

He sat down on the couch and leaned back in a relaxed manner with his arm stretched across the carved wood back. "Gigot sleeves?"

"Yes. See how they're wide and rounded at the shoulder. Then they taper down to a snug fit at the wrist. They're sometimes called leg-of-mutton sleeves."

"A rather unappealing name, don't you think? Sheep's leg sleeves."

Elise shrugged. "I guess so. But I like gigot sleeves."

Jordan nodded. "Then so do I. But I don't like that dress much. It doesn't have a waist."

Elise replaced the dress, happy that they had made at least some progress toward a choice. She pulled another dress out. "This has a very narrow, fitted silhouette. It has the gigot sleeves and a high neckline. This is made of silk charmeuse with a Venise lace overlay."

Jordan considered the dress, then looked up at her. "What do you think?"

"It isn't the dress that I would choose for myself, but with Abby's figure, it would probably be a perfect choice."

"Which dress would you choose?" His gaze was penetrating.

Elise drew the gown out from behind the others. "This one," she answered, her voice breathy with sentiment. "This is silk shantung. It has a basque waist. See, it's fitted and comes to a point in the front. The bodice and sleeves have an Alençon lace overlay and are hand beaded with these tiny pearls." She swept her arm under the dress, dragging it along the floor to show off the five-foot train. "And it has a sweetheart neckline. See how it looks like the top of a heart." Elise pointed to the low neckline, her fingers following the gentle curves at the front of the dress. "And at the shoulders are these roses with little sprays of pearls." She touched the roses reverently.

"And it has gigot sleeves," Jordan added.

"Yes, it has gigot sleeves." She smiled, her eyes still fixed on the dress.

"I like it," Jordan said firmly. "That's the one."

Elise looked up at him in shock, an uncontrollable rush of resentment coursing through her. "No!" she heard herself say. This was *her* dress. This was the gown *she* would walk down the aisle in. It wasn't meant for Abby, it was meant for *her*.

"No?" Jordan asked. "I thought you liked the dress."

"I—I do. But I don't think it would be right for Abby."

"I think it would be perfect for my bride. But before I make a final decision, I'd like to see it on."

"On?"

"Yes, I want you to put it on. It's hard to tell what it will look like when it's hanging on the hanger."

Elise shook her head. "I can't."

"Why not? Is it the wrong size?" Jordan stood up and grabbed the tag that dangled from the sleeve. "It's a size ten. Perfect. Go ahead, try it on. I'll wait here."

"But—"

"Go ahead," he said, pushing her out the door, the dress clutched in her arms. "Before I spend—" he grabbed the tag again "—four thousand dollars on a wedding gown, I want to see what it's going to look like on my bride."

Elise stepped into the adjoining fitting room, closed the door behind her and slowly sank onto a reproduction French chaise. She hugged the dress to her and the crisp skirt rustled against her legs.

She was torn, one part of her wanting to put the dress on and the other wanting to hide it from Jordan, hoping desperately to convince him not to buy it. She had been tempted to try the gown on every time she walked into the shop, but had refused to give in to the fantasy. What good would it do, dreaming of a wedding that might never happen? Though she was a pure romantic, her romanticism did have its limits. She was practical enough to realize that without a man in her life, there would be no hope for a wedding.

Yes, she was also practical. And she was smart enough to separate fact from fantasy. So why not try the dress on? Why not enjoy the moment?

"Is that the one?"

Elise looked up to see Sheila standing in the doorway. She nodded and Sheila grinned.

"Nice choice. Big commission. Why don't you give me the dress and I'll hang it up? Then we can go write up the sale."

"He wants me to try it on first," Elise said dismally. "He's waiting in the other room." Elise stood and began to unbutton her blouse with numb fingers. She pulled off the rest of her clothes, letting them drop in a heap at her feet on top of her discarded shoes. With Sheila's help, she silently slipped the dress over her head, her grim expression staring back at her from the floor-to-ceiling mirrors.

As Sheila worked the tiny buttons from the small of her back to her nape, Elise felt the bodice gradually mold itself to her figure. She stared at the reflection of her face, refusing to shift her gaze to the dress.

"Stunning," Sheila said in a tone of genuine admiration. "Let me get a veil." She returned moments later with a fingertip veil that flounced and cascaded from a cap of pearls. She pulled Elise's hair back into a knot and secured it with bobby pins, then placed the veil on Elise's head and anchored it with two combs.

"Exquisite!" she declared, sighing as she straightened the veil. "It's like the dress was made for you."

Elise finally let her gaze drift downward over her reflection. She could barely believe the vision that met her eyes. For the first time in her life she felt truly beautiful. She watched as Sheila fastened a string of pearls around her neck. Elise reached up to run her fingers along the cool ridges of the necklace. Her fingertips came to rest at the base of her throat where her pulse drummed frantically.

"Shoes," Sheila muttered. She rushed out again and returned with a box under her arm. Kneeling, she found Elise's toes under the voluminous skirt and slipped a pair of beaded slippers onto her feet. The shoes were a size too big, but the design was a perfect match for the dress.

"There you are," Sheila proclaimed with a flourish of her hand. "The ideal bride."

Elise graced her with a wavering smile. "I'm afraid I'm only the stand-in model for the ideal bride."

"Oh, who cares," Sheila said with a laugh. "We've been playing dress-up since we were little girls. It was fun then and it's even more fun now. So enjoy it."

Sheila took a final look, her hands smoothing a fold in the skirt before she left Elise alone in the fitting room. Glancing at her image once more, Elise drew a nervous breath, then walked out the door.

She was completely unprepared for Jordan's reaction. He looked up from his file folder. His gaze traveled slowly from her toes to her face. His eyes met hers and they stared at each other for a long moment. The space between them crackled with a current of tightly leashed excitement.

Jordan stood up, his gaze still locked on her face. "You look . . . incredible," he said as he let out tightly held breath.

Elise dipped her head, as a blush crept up her cheeks. "Thank you," she said softly. "I feel incredible."

"Turn around," Jordan ordered. "Slowly."

Her legs wobbled as she began an agonizing pirouette. She had almost completed her turn, when her eyes caught Jordan's again and she stumbled. Her foot twisted out of the oversize shoe, and she found herself listing precariously to one side.

In a swift, sure movement, Jordan stepped to her side and grabbed her waist.

She smiled in gratitude, the heat from his fingers burning through the heavy fabric of her bodice. "I—I lost my shoe." She searched the space under her skirts for the missing slipper, sliding her unshod foot over the carpet in a clumsy quest.

"Let me get it," Jordan offered. He bent down on one knee to lift her skirts up and retrieve the shoe, then held her foot in his hand and slid the slipper back onto her foot.

To steady herself Elise placed her hands on his broad shoulders, her sensitized fingers feeling the bunched muscle through the fabric of his suit.

Her breath caught in her throat as his firm fingers wrapped around her ankle. Slowly, very tentatively, he ran his hand from her ankle to her knee. She suppressed a tiny moan that threatened to escape from her throat.

He looked up at her. "There, that's better."

"Yes," she whispered in a wavering voice, meeting his gaze. "Much better." Her fingers clenched unconsciously and she felt Jordan's shoulders stiffen in response.

He stood, then suddenly turned from her and walked across the room. For a long moment, he didn't move. Then, with a muttered oath, he turned back and strode toward her, his expression grim and determined. He pulled her against his hard body and his lips descended over hers to cover her mouth.

In a single, shattering explosion, her mind lost the ability to reason and she opened her mouth to his. His probing tongue tangled with hers, sending tremors of delight to her core. She abandoned herself to his kiss and let the need wash over her in waves, pushing and pulling and driving her to seek more.

He groaned against her mouth and pulled her hips firmly against his, straining through the layers of silk and petticoats.

Suddenly, reality struck her, a sharp slap in the face, a chilling douse of icy water. She opened her eyes wide and tore her mouth from his.

"No," she said, her voice a strangled cry.

He opened his eyes and she could see fire burning in their depths. "Don't stop me, Elise," he growled, his words more a warning than a request. "Let it happen."

"I can't," she pleaded, her voice barely audible. "You can't. You're engaged. This is wrong. You don't love me—you love her." She buried her face in his shoulder.

"I don't love her," Jordan said in a matter-of-fact tone.

Elise snapped her head up and stared at him, too astonished to speak. She finally found her voice, but her words came out in a whisper of disbelief. "You can't mean that."

"It's true. I don't love her." He paused. "And she doesn't love me."

A tiny spark of relief touched Elise's heart at his words, but she stopped the reaction immediately. It didn't matter. Jordan was still engaged. "Why are you getting married if you don't love each other?"

"These are the nineties, Elise. Love isn't a requirement for marriage. People marry for other reasons all the time."

Elise stepped away from him, hurt by his patronizing tone. "What other reasons are there?"

"Security, stability. I'm thirty-eight years old. It's time I got married and started a family." He shrugged. "I have a great deal of money. My wife will be able to buy whatever her heart desires."

Elise felt her anger rise. How could he be so cold and unfeeling? "You think your money really matters? What if her heart desires love?"

"It doesn't and neither does she. She knows exactly what to expect from this marriage and she's satisfied. She's getting what she wants and I'm getting what I want."

"Then why this elaborate wedding?" Elise demanded, indignation coloring her voice. "Why this?" She held out her skirts. "It seems like a ridiculous waste of money for a marriage in name only."

"It's necessary," Jordan stated.

Elise shook her head in bewilderment. He was making a mockery of everything she believed in, her dreams, her career, her life.

"And I suppose this is perfectly acceptable to you," she said.

"What?"

"This . . . this episode, this . . . lapse in judgment."

"Yes," he said with a wry expression. "I'd have to say that it is quite acceptable."

Elise's fingers clenched into fists around the crisp fabric of her skirt. "Where do you think this will lead? Do you expect me to just happily agree to carry on some tawdry little affair behind your fiancée's back? Is that why you sent the flowers—to smooth the way for this seduction attempt?"

Jordan frowned. "That's not the way it is. I sent you the flowers . . ." He shook his head. "Hell, I don't even know why I sent the flowers anymore. But it wasn't part of some scheme, if that's what you think. Elise, you can't deny that there's something going on between us. I want—no, I need to find out what it is."

"And what would Abby say?"

Jordan's features tensed, yet she saw indecision color his expression. He rubbed his brow with his fingers and paused, as if considering his next words very carefully before uttering them. "Abby would say nothing because Abby doesn't—"

"No," Elise warned, holding up her hand to stop his words. "Don't you dare speak for her again."

"Elise, let me explain. Abby doesn't—"

"I don't want to hear your lies!" she shouted, covering her ears.

Jordan grabbed her wrists and pulled her hands away from her ears. "Then maybe it's time for the truth," he growled. "I want you, and I know you want me. How's that for the truth?"

Elise glared at him. "No, I don't want you!"

He yanked her to him and his mouth covered hers again, this time in a rough, demanding kiss. Elise pushed at his chest, but he tightened his hold on her. Her body screamed for his touch, begged to let him continue, but her mind refused to give in. It was wrong!

He dragged his lips to her throat, murmuring, "Tell me you don't want this, Elise."

Tears burned at the corners of her eyes, but she blinked them back, drawing on her resolve. "It doesn't make any difference what I want. You're an engaged man."

With one final burst of defiance, she shoved against his chest, catching him unaware. Then she grabbed her skirts and ran from his presence. Racing through the showroom, she wove her way around the dress racks scattered across the dark salon. Maneuvering in the heavy dress was difficult and as she turned sharply, she stumbled.

Elise kicked off the shoes and and reached down to grab the train and throw it over her arm. Jordan emerged from the fitting room, ran his fingers through his hair, then started in her direction.

Elise grabbed the shoes and stood up. "Stay right there," she commanded.

Jordan paused. "Elise, we need to talk. I want to explain."

"I don't want to hear what you have to say."

"Dammit, Elise, running away from this is not going to make it go away." He started toward her again.

"I said, stay there!" she cried. Acting instinctively, she threw one of the beaded slippers at him. It sailed across the showroom, missing Jordan by a good three feet. He continued in her direction and she hurled another warning shot. This time, the slipper came dangerously close to his ear.

"You're out of ammunition, Elise. Now it's time to negotiate."

Elise took a tentative step back. "There won't be any negotiation. My mind is made up."

He looked at her with a tight expression. "I'm not going to stop until we—"

She held up her hand. "No! What happened in there was wrong. I was wrong to allow it. And you were wrong to begin it." With that, she spun on her heel and headed toward the front door.

She passed Sheila on her way and before she could make good her escape, Sheila grabbed at her elbow. "Elise, where are you going?" Elise eluded her grasp and pushed open the door of the shop.

"Hey, what about the dress?" Sheila cried.

"We'll take it," Elise shouted back. With that, she ran down the steps and out to the street, her skirt held high and her stocking feet tripping across the cold concrete.

With a frantic wave, she hailed a passing cab. It screeched to a halt in front of her. The cabbie slid across the front seat, rolled down the window and grinned at her. "You left him at the altar, right, sweetheart?" He glanced down. "Let me guess. Cold feet?" He laughed at his joke.

"Very funny," she snapped as she yanked the door open and tumbled inside.

"So, now that you've dumped the creep, I've got a live-in brother-in-law that's looking for a wife. No reason for that pretty dress to go to waste."

"Just shut up and drive," Elise replied. She gave the driver her address, then watched the door of the bridal shop, hoping that Jordan had decided against following her.

The cabbie punched the accelerator and Elise was thrown back against the seat. She closed her eyes and tipped her head back, steadfastly refusing to give in to the tears that threatened.

Good Lord, what had she done? She had kissed him. Even worse, she had enjoyed it.

How could she have allowed herself to lose control, to find herself in the arms of an engaged man, and a client at that? And to believe that her feelings were merely a harmless infatuation. She now realized she'd felt more than infatuation when he'd held her in his embrace. She was falling in love with Jordan Prentiss.

Elise groaned and covered her eyes with her arm. Deep in a hidden corner of her mind, she had secretly harbored a fantasy that she was to be Jordan's bride. And through it all, she had planned his wedding as if it were *her* wedding, as well. Her favorite flowers, her favorite music, even her favorite bridal gown. Every choice had been made with her own tastes in mind.

And suddenly the fantasy had sprung to life before her eyes. Jordan wanted her as much as she wanted him.

It was bound to happen. The attraction had been there from the start. She had just refused to recognize it. But was that all her fault? The mysterious Abby hadn't donated a single ounce of help in planning the wedding. Her absence had provided ample opportunity for them to get carried away with each other.

And Jordan was also partially to blame. Elise had simply made a slight error in judgment. She had let herself get caught up with a picture perfect wedding and a handsome and undeniably sexy groom.

And now the dream wedding had turned into a nightmare. She was supposed to give her clients a "happily ever after." But instead she was standing directly between a man and the woman he planned to marry. In any other situation she would have bolted, but she couldn't afford to give this job up. Besides losing a great deal of money, quitting at this late date could ruin her professional reputation.

Her head told her she couldn't quit. But her heart told her she certainly couldn't go on.

5

JORDAN STRODE to the front window of the shop and caught a glimpse of Elise's bare foot and the lacy white hem of the dress before the cab door slammed shut. When he stepped out onto the sidewalk a moment later, the cab was halfway down the block, its glowing red taillights disappearing into the night.

"Damn," he muttered. Motionless, he stared down the street until the cold began to seep into his consciousness. Then, with another curse, he turned and walked back inside the shop.

He headed directly to the fitting room, ignoring the shop owner's quizzical look, and slammed the door behind him. Pacing the perimeter of the tiny room, he tried to repair his shredded self-control.

What had possessed him to kiss her? He knew Elise well enough to have predicted her reaction, yet he'd still felt compelled to test her resolve. And she had been wearing that damned dress. All he had wanted was to see what she looked like in it, to appease his curiosity and enjoy her incredible beauty. And the dandelions? He had rationalized the gift as a mere thank-you for her help and attention. But now he realized that he had sent them with the hope that they would pave the way to something more. In truth, he had fantasized that once confronted with his desire for her, she would happily capitulate and accept a simple affair with no strings attached. Since Elise, with her romantic ideals and storybook view of marriage, was not appropriate wife material for him, a discreet liaison was the next best option.

But if he looked deep into his heart he knew the prospect of a discreet affair was as distasteful to him as the suggestion would have been to Elise. But why? He'd always been satisfied with these types of casual arrangements in the past.

Yet whenever he was around Elise, he found himself wanting more, throwing caution out the window to consider what life could be like with her at his side. All common sense fled when he looked into her wide, expectant gaze, and he found himself savoring the possibilities of the two of them, together, always. He had kissed her, and in that single instant, his self-control had shattered into a million irretrievable pieces.

How could he possibly consider marriage to a woman who had such a disconcerting and dangerous effect on him? In the rush to satisfy his craving for her, he had almost admitted the truth about his lack of a bride. Elise had a way of making him want to open the doors to his soul and show the secrets inside. She made him want to believe that endless love and absolute trust between a man and a woman were achievable. She made him want to take a risk.

Jordan sank down on the settee and, with an impatient sigh, raked his hands through his hair. How had such a simple plan gone so far astray? He had set his goals, arranged his priorities and developed a clear strategy. Yet nothing was going right. Finding a wife should have been no more difficult that completing a basic business acquisition. Locate the target, analyze the target's weaknesses, attack those weaknesses and take control. Just where had his plan gone wrong?

For starters, the target phase had fallen woefully short. He hadn't found a woman who came close to meeting his criteria. It wasn't like he was asking for perfection. He just wanted someone practical, level-headed and logical.

A woman nothing like Elise.

Jordan tipped his head back and drew a ragged breath. Somewhere along the line, he had lost sight of his primary purpose. And it had happened right around the time he had met Elise Sinclair. From the start, she had been a wrench in his plans; she had turned a simple process into a chaotic mess.

He hadn't counted on this overwhelming desire he felt for her. He wanted her, completely and absolutely, without regard for the consequences. To hell with his plan, forget the wife, forget the wedding. Right now, his one-and-only goal was to bury himself in her warmth, to take her body and to possess her heart.

But that was the essence of the problem, this over-powering need to have her heart as his own. He wanted her love and loyalty, yet he knew he couldn't give her the same in return. All he could give her would be what his money could buy: jewelry, a huge house, fancy clothing . . . dandelions in the dead of winter. He imagined her reaction to the flowers. He saw her smile, heard her gentle laugh. God, how he loved to see her happy. But how long would it be before that smile vanished and that laughter disappeared? How long until she felt trapped in a one-sided relationship, devoid of a shared love and commitment?

He had watched his mother's smiles and laughter disappear as his father had become more distant and preoccupied with work. All she had wanted was his father's love, yet he had seemed oblivious to her needs until it was too late. She had gone looking for what was missing in her life and had found it with another man. Would Elise do the same?

A raging flood of jealousy coursed through his veins. Once Elise was his, she would be his and his alone. For when he had something in his hands of great value, he protected it above all else. Until now, only his company had deserved such a single-minded defense. But if Elise became his, he would allow no one to take her from him.

Ruthless. The word had been applied to him more than once and he took pride in the description. He approached each corporate battle with cool precision and a deliberate lack of emotion, for emotion had no place in his business life—or in his personal life. Misplaced loyalties and sentimental choices had destroyed others, making their companies vulnerable to people like Jordan. They were fools, all of them. Emotional fools.

But wasn't what he was feeling for Elise coming dangerously close to real emotion? Jealousy, frustration, desire. All of these were feelings that could lead him to lose control.

Jordan snapped his briefcase closed and pulled on his coat. He needed to devise a solution to his problem, a damage-control plan that would put his search for a wife back on track.

He searched his mind for a strategy as he settled the bill for the wedding dress. By the time he got into his car, he was still groping for a game plan. Ten minutes later, as he drove through the traffic on Michigan Avenue, he realized that any plan to put Elise Sinclair completely out of his life was not going to be simple.

He wanted her and he would stop at nothing to have her. Yet he was at a complete loss. He hadn't a clue as to how to go about making her his. In the past, he had diligently avoided the emotional aspects of relationships, leaving him with no understanding of the complicated mechanics that could exist between a man and a woman. And now, when some insight into the tender side of a woman's psyche might help his cause, he had nowhere to turn, no experience to draw upon.

Jordan circled the block and headed toward Lake Shore Drive. As his Mercedes sped north, he opened the sunroof and turned up the radio, hoping the drive would clear his head.

Damn Elise Sinclair! Damn her lovely face and her expressive eyes, her lush figure and her kissable mouth.

And damn him for letting her into his life.

FROM THE SILENT DEPTHS of the house, the mantel clock chimed, bringing Elise's foggy mind back to reality. She groaned and pulled herself up from where she lay sprawled in the middle of her parlor floor, a quilt wrapped around her shoulders. In one hand, she held a glass of wine and in the other, her cordless telephone. The billowing skirt and petticoats of the bridal dress surrounded her like a fluffy white cloud.

She was trapped. Caught in the confines of a dreamy dress that had turned into a straitjacket. She put her wine and the phone down beside her, then crooked her arm behind her back and tried once again to unfasten the row of tiny buttons between her shoulder blades. But her grasping fingertips could reach just so far. Clorinda and Thisbe observed her from an overstuffed chair, reveling in her plight and smiling their smug little cat smiles.

"You think this is funny, huh?" she muttered, glaring at the cats. "As I recall, you didn't think it was so funny when you locked yourselves in the linen closet."

Maybe she should call 911. Or the fire department. If someone didn't rescue her soon from this four-thousand-dollar prison of silk and lace, she would have to cut the gown off her body. She grabbed the phone, dialed Dona's number and waited for the message on her friend's answering machine to run through.

"Hi, it's me again," Elise said with desperation in her voice. "Where are you? It's midnight. Please come over here as soon as you get in. I need your help." She switched off the phone, picked up her wineglass and gulped down the last of the warm Chardonnay, then wiped the back of her hand across her lips. With a deep sigh, she stretched out on the floor. The ceiling seemed to slowly rotate above her and she closed her eyes. The combination of two glasses of wine and sheer emotional exhaustion had made her numb and a little light-headed.

Her mind drifted back, as it had over and over in the past three hours, replaying the disastrous turn of events in the bridal salon. She recalled each moment with such clarity that she wondered if it would ever be possible to banish the memories from her mind. The warm spread of Jordan's fingers across her back, his firm mouth covering hers, the musky scent of his cologne, the vibration of a moan deep in his throat.

Though she tried to deny her feelings at every turn, she knew another full-fledged assault on her already shaky moral standards would end in her surrender to Jordan Prentiss. She wanted him. It no longer mattered that he was engaged. She wanted him with a passion that blotted out the real world, leaving them alone, together, in a fantasy world where there were no barriers between them.

What she felt for him was like nothing she had ever experienced before—every nerve in her body was alert to his touch, her pulse pounded in a maddening rhythm. But her mind was at war with her heart. Love, hate, desire, denial. Wrong, right, pleasure, pain. And surrounding it all, a whirlpool of confusion.

He had said he wanted her, but where did his feelings begin and end? Was it just lust that drove him to kiss her? Or was there true emotion behind his actions? Did he care for her? Did he love her? Would he break his engagement?

Elise drew in a deep breath, then released it slowly. It had happened before. She had planned more than one wedding that had ended long before the altar. Engagements were broken all the time, for any number of reasons—cold feet, incompatibility, another man... another woman. Though canceled wedding plans were a tremendous bother, she always felt relieved that a mistake had not been made, that love and commitment had not been compromised. A marriage without love was inconceivable to her, a travesty of the wedding vows, a lie, a sham.

But wasn't that what Jordan was embarking upon? He had spoken of his marriage like a business deal, cold and calculated, an exchange of money for services rendered. Poor Abby, she thought. Caught in a loveless union.

No! She couldn't feel sorry for her. If Jordan was telling the truth, Abby was well aware of what she was stepping into. They were consenting adults, after all. And they were both getting what they wanted out of the deal, as mercenary as it might seem to her eyes.

Who was she to judge? She was only their wedding consultant, hired to turn the most important day of their lives into the most memorable day, also. But she couldn't do it, not anymore. Not after what she had experienced with Jordan.

If he planned to proceed with his wedding plans, she would be forced to quit. She couldn't watch silently as the man she was falling in love with married someone else. There would be pain, but no guilt.

But what if Jordan chose to cancel the wedding and break his engagement? This might seem like the ideal situation. But maybe Jordan was wrong and Abby did love him. If he chose Elise, then there would be guilt, but no pain.

Either way, Elise knew her life would never be the same.

The shrill sound of the doorbell jolted her upright. Dona! She struggled to her feet, dragging the quilt with her, and stumbled over her skirts in her haste to reach the foyer. As she yanked the door open, the cold winter wind swirled in around her. Her smile froze as she came face-to-face with Jordan Prentiss.

He stood on her stoop, a grim look on his face. He wore no coat; his hands were shoved into his pants pockets and his suit-jacket collar was turned up against the wind. His silk tie was loosened, his dark hair windblown and wild. Elise was momentarily stunned at his appearance; his usual impeccable grooming was nowhere to be found and his practiced facade of complete control was gone.

She reversed her motion and swung the door shut, but at the last second, he braced his foot against it and forced it open a crack.

She peeked through at him. "Why are you here?"

"Elise, we have to talk. Let me in—it's cold out here."

"Answer one question. Do you still plan to go through with this wedding?"

"Yes."

His baldly stated reply was like a slap in the face. She shoved against the door with her shoulder and flipped the dead bolt. Had she really expected any other answer? A wave of self-recrimination washed over her. When was she going to learn? Love did not conquer all. There was no such thing as love at first sight. And love was definitely not a many-splendored thing.

The doorbell sounded again, this time more insistently.

"Just go away," she shouted through the door. "I don't want to talk to you. I don't ever want to see you again. I quit. You can find someone else to plan this wedding."

"Let me in, Elise." She could hear the rising irritation in his voice. "I have something I need to say to you. I'll stand out here all night if I have to." He pounded on the door and rang the bell again. "If you don't let me in, I'll kick this door down."

Elise quickly reconsidered his demand. Could he really kick the door down? She'd seen it in the movies all the time, but had never believed anyone would attempt it in real life, except maybe the police. Though the threat conjured up very romantic images, the thought of her lovely old oak door splintering on its hinges moved her to action and she reluctantly obeyed his demand.

Jordan stalked through the foyer and into the parlor, heading for the fireplace. Finding no warmth there, he began to pace the room restlessly, rubbing his hands together.

"It's colder in here than it is outside," he muttered, glancing her way.

Elise watched him from the parlor door. She wrapped the quilt more tightly around her, hoping to quell the nervous flutter in her stomach and the goose bumps that accompanied it. "The boiler's broken again," she murmured. She took a deep breath, then met his gaze squarely. "Whatever you have to say is not going to change my mind. I still quit."

He ran his hands through his hair, his pale eyes intensely blue. "Elise, I've made a decision. I want you to marry me."

"Didn't you hear what I just said?" Her voice rose in volume. "I quit. You can take your wedding to another consultant. I'll even help you find my replacement."

"I want you to marry me, Elise," he said, enunciating very clearly, as if she were hard of hearing. "I want you to be my wife."

"I can hear perfectly well," she answered, crossing her arms in a defensive posture. "You're the one who appears to be deaf. I said, I—" She looked at him, dumbfounded, as the meaning of his words sank in. No, she couldn't have heard right! "You want me to be your what?"

"My wife."

The two simple words set up a pounding in her chest and she groped for a logical reply. His wife? "But...but you're already engaged. What about Abby?"

"Abby's a dog."

A stab of anger shot through her. "How can you say that about the woman you're going to marry? How can you be so cruel?" Earlier, he had described Abby as beautiful. Come to think of it, he had said Abby resembled Elise. And now, he was comparing Abby with a dog? Elise felt a sting from the insult.

"Elise, there is no Abby." He rubbed his forehead in a way that had already become familiar to her, an action that signaled his frustration. "No, that's not quite true. There was, but she's dead."

Elise's brow furrowed in confusion. This conversation was becoming more bizarre by the moment. "You've been planning a wedding to a dead per—" A shattering feeling of alarm raced through her. "Oh, my God. You didn't. You—you murdered her!"

Elise backed slowly out of the doorway. But her cautious retreat from a man who could very likely be a homicidal maniac was stopped when her heels tangled in her skirts. She cried out as she fell squarely on her backside in the middle of the foyer. Jordan appeared above her and she scooted away from him until he grabbed her arms and hauled her to her feet.

"Elise, what has gotten into you? I didn't murder anyone. Abby died of old age when I was fifteen. She was my cocker spaniel. You wanted a name and that's the first name that came to mind."

Her thoughts remained a jumble. "You're planning to marry a dead cocker spaniel?" She tried to wade through her bewilderment to understand what he was saying. He wasn't a murderer; he was a . . . a . . . well, she wasn't quite sure what the term was for a man who intended to marry an animal, and a dead one at that. "This is sick. Get out of my house before I call the police."

"Listen to me. There is no Abby. There is no fiancée. There never was." He grabbed her hands and pulled her toward the couch. Hesitantly she sat down beside him, keeping a careful distance. "It was a lie," he continued.

"All part of a very complicated plan. And a very stupid plan now that I look back on it."

Elise frowned. She wondered whether forgoing the two glasses of Chardonnay earlier would have made a difference in her understanding of this conversation. Somehow she didn't think so. "Why am I planning a wedding if there's no fiancée?"

"I know this sounds strange, but the bottom line is, I need a wife." Jordan took a deep breath before continuing. His next words came out in a rush. "You and I seem to have some sort of attraction to each other. I should have acknowledged it right away. But I've never been good at this sort of thing. I need a wife, so it might as well be you."

"As opposed to a dog?"

Jordan sighed. "Forget the damn dog. Will you or will you not marry me?"

For a moment, she was speechless, staring at him through uncomprehending eyes. Then she found her voice. "Just like that? We barely know each other."

"I know, I know. But that really doesn't make any difference." He held up his hand to stop any further comment on her part. "Just listen to the whole deal before you make up your mind. If I don't get married, I'm probably going to lose my company. My cousin Edward has been maneuvering for control of BabyLove and he's managed to convince the board of directors that I don't represent the family image that our company needs to convey to the public. I really don't think my marital status has anything to do with this shift in loyalties, but they're going to use it to force me out. They've decided they want a more stable, conservative president. To them, marriage means stability."

"A marriage proposal is supposed to be romantic," she mumbled as she studied her fingers.

Jordan continued his explanation, not hearing her softly spoken words. "I decided that a quick marriage would be the best defense. I called you to begin plans for the wedding and I started looking for a suitable bride. But things just haven't gone as smoothly as I anticipated. I'm not quite sure why, but they haven't."

"You're supposed to get down on one knee and confess your undying love for me." She talked to herself, aware that Jordan was too intent on his sales pitch to listen.

"I'm offering you a tremendous opportunity. I'm a wealthy man, Elise. I can give you anything you want. You'll never have to work again."

"And a ring," she said wistfully, glancing up at his determined expression. "There should be an engagement ring. In a little black velvet box."

Jordan looked at her strangely, finally acknowledging her words. "Yes, of course. You can go out and buy the most expensive ring in Chicago. There are a lot of other benefits involved here, too. You'll have a housekeeper so you'll never have to worry about housework. After we have children—we need to have children, at least two. A boy and a girl would be nice, a boy first and then a girl. Of course we'll hire a nanny. You'll have a very comfortable life, Elise. It's a very generous offer."

"This isn't romantic at all," she said, shaking her head. He had their entire life mapped out like one of his business plans.

"Of course, if the marriage doesn't work out, you'll be well compensated. So you see, there's really no risk involved. Either way, you come out much better financially than you are right now." He paused. "And I get to keep my company."

"This isn't the way it's supposed to be," she protested, twisting her fingers together nervously.

"Elise, whatever it is that you want, it's yours. We can put all the details into a prenuptial agreement if it would make you feel better. All you have to do is ask."

She focused on his eyes. "Do you love me?"

Jordan's expression remained remote, but she could see his reaction in the shift of his gaze, as if he were weighing the merits of a lie versus the truth. "Elise, I think it's important that we always be honest with each other."

"Do you love me?" she repeated more firmly, already knowing the answer.

"No, I don't. But that doesn't really matter. It doesn't impact the problem at hand."

Elise shook her head. "It has everything in the world to do with the problem at hand. How can you propose marriage to a woman you don't love? And knowing that, how can you expect me to accept?"

"I think you're confusing two very different issues here. Marriage is a legal agreement. Love is an emotional commitment. The two can be mutually exclusive. Elise, we're attracted to each other—that's a start. But I won't confuse lust with love."

Elise wondered if she could say the same. Was what she felt for Jordan actually the beginnings of love or merely a nasty case of lust? "They may not really be that far apart."

Jordan shook his head. "I'd be lying to you. I'm just not capable of that type of emotional investment."

Elise felt her temper rise. "You talk about love like it's some kind of business liability. You're writing it off like a bad debt, before you've even tried to collect."

"Elise, I've explained the deal. You know all the terms. Will you marry me?"

She shook her head indignantly, her answer coming to her lips without a second thought. "No, Jordan. I will not marry you."

Jordan stared at her, his handsome features frozen in a mask of utter disbelief. "No? You're refusing me?"

Elise nodded.

He jumped up from the couch and began to pace the room again. "Why?" he shouted. "What the hell is wrong with me? I'm wealthy. I'm not a drunk or a cheat. I'm a good-looking guy." He slapped his palms on his chest. "I'm Chicago's most eligible bachelor! Women like me. You like me, and don't try to deny it."

Elise fought an outrageous urge to laugh. She had suspected Jordan had an ego, but she had never before seen it manifest itself. "Just because you're the most eligible, doesn't make you the most suitable. And I'm sure women do like you, Jordan," she agreed, "but that's not enough to base a marriage on. At least not for me."

Jordan stood before the fireplace, gripping the mantel, his back to Elise. "Suddenly, it's like I've contracted the plague. Before I decided I needed a wife, I had all the women I could handle. Now I can't seem to find an eligible woman in the entire city of Chicago, not one who's smart enough to see the up side of marrying me."

"Maybe it's your approach," she shot back.

Jordan turned to her with a look of surprise. "My approach? What's wrong with my approach?" He returned to the couch and sat down beside her, his gaze

curious. "I'm very straightforward about what I want
and what my wife can expect." He laughed dryly.
"Women are always talking about honesty in a relationship and I'm being very honest. Are you saying I
should lie?"

"No, of course not. I'm just saying marriage to you
would be a little easier to ... accept if you offered
something beyond basic financial security. Your proposal sounded more like a retirement plan than a romantic declaration. Marriage is not a business deal. It's
more than that. Much, much more."

"Like what?" he asked sullenly.

"Affection and trust. Commitment. These things
aren't available on demand, Jordan. They take time.
People don't just jump right into marriage. There's a
logical reason for a period of courtship. It gives a man
and a woman time to learn about each other."

Jordan considered her suggestions for only a moment before continuing their debate. "But I haven't got
time," he answered. "The wedding has to take place as
scheduled. I need to find a way to bypass that ... that
whatever you call it."

"Courtship phase," Elise repeated. "But that's the
most romantic part of a relationship. There aren't very
many women I know who would want to give that up."

"Ha! So we're back to that again. Romance."

Elise shrugged. "You have to admit, your proposal
was lacking in that area."

Jordan studied her closely. "So if I would have been
more romantic you would have accepted?"

"No," Elise answered stubbornly. "But I might have
given it a second thought."

His expression turned hard and a muscle twitched in
his jaw. "I knew this wouldn't work."

"Well, I think we had better cancel the wedding plans. I really don't think it's possible for—"

"No," Jordan stated coldly, turning away from her to pace the room. "I have to get married. If you won't marry me, then you have to help me."

"Help you what?"

He turned and fixed her with a pointed stare. "Find a wife."

Elise's jaw dropped and she gasped, unable to believe what he was saying. Just moments ago, he had asked her to marry him and now he acted as if the words had never passed his lips, as if she were no more than a passing whim in his grand plan. He expected her to help him find a wife? He had to be joking.

"I don't know why I didn't think of it before. You know all about romance and you can give me insights into the tangle of the female mind. With your help I can intensify my efforts and breeze right through this courtship phase."

Elise's heart constricted in her chest. It was as if he had suddenly turned to ice, colder and harder than the man she first met on her front stoop. He was serious. And he obviously had no idea how she felt about him or he wouldn't have asked such a thing. She crossed the room to toy with a vase of silk flowers on an ornate Victorian fern stand. "Jordan, really, I don't think—"

He followed and stood behind her. "If you help me and I manage to pull this off by my deadline, I'll double your fee. And if the wedding doesn't happen as planned, I'll give you your regular fee, anyway. It's a generous offer, Elise. Think about it."

She turned to look at him. Her eyes skimmed the sculpted contours of his face, a face that had haunted her thoughts from the day she'd met him. She was tempted to reach out and warm his frozen expression with her touch, but she resisted the impulse, balling her hands into tight fists, instead.

Could she do it? Could she bury her silly feelings for this man and help him find a wife? After all, there was no hope for a relationship with him; that fact was painfully clear. He had already forgotten his offer to her, brushing it off like a passing fancy.

Jordan Prentiss hadn't a clue as to what she needed in a husband and she was a fool ever to think that he could make her happy. So why not take him up on his offer? She could certainly use the money and she had already invested too much time in this wedding to let it go now. A new roof, a new boiler and utility payments were part of real life. Her infatuation with Jordan was simply a dream.

Elise bit her bottom lip, then nodded hesitantly. "All right," she said in a thin voice. "I'll do it."

Jordan nodded curtly. "We have a deal, then."

"Yes," she said, trying to force a bit of conviction into her reply. "We have a deal."

"All right." Jordan turned and walked to the door. "I'll call you tomorrow and we'll set up a schedule of . . . romance consultations." He grabbed the doorknob. "This will work. I know it will."

He turned to her once more, his gaze catching her wide eyes. Elise thought she saw a flash of regret cross his face. "You do look incredible in that dress," he murmured.

Elise swallowed convulsively and smiled. "Thank you."

"Why are you still wearing it?"

A blush warmed her cheeks. "I can't seem to get myself out of it. It's the buttons. They're so tiny and I can't reach . . ."

Jordan strode back into the parlor and firmly took hold of her shoulders, then turned her around so that her back faced him. With deft fingers, he released each pearl button from its tiny loop. His thumbs grazed her bare back and sent tingles of sensation shooting to her toes and fingertips. As the last button was undone and the dress threatened to fall from her shoulders, she clutched her hands to her chest and spun around to face him.

For a fleeting moment, she caught an expression of pain on his face, but then it disappeared, replaced by his normal detached facade.

"I'll call you," he said in a subdued voice.

"Fine," she answered, watching his return to the door.

He didn't turn back this time, only paused a moment before saying a blunt and businesslike "Good night."

As the door closed behind him, Elise sank to the floor, the dress ballooning out around her. She grabbed a throw pillow from the couch and buried her face in it. When she raised her head, she saw Clorinda and Thisbe sitting in front of her, eyeing the pearls scattered across the skirt of the bridal gown. She tossed the pillow at them and sent the pair retreating to a safe distance across the room.

In her wildest dreams, she had never imagined a marriage proposal like the one Jordan had made to her. Nor had she ever dreamed that the one and only time a proposal was offered, she would flatly turn it down.

THE RESTAURANT on the sixth floor of the Bloomingdale's building was nearly empty when Elise arrived.
She chose a small table along the floor-to-ceiling windows and watched the midmorning traffic from high
above Michigan Avenue as she sipped at her coffee. She
stifled a yawn behind her hand and rubbed her scratchy
eyes, wondering how much sleep she had actually gotten the night before. As far as she could recall, it had
been less than an hour. A frantic two a.m. call from
Dona had interrupted her only slumber.

She waited patiently for the caffeine to kick in, hoping that she would recover some of her faculties before
her appointment downtown with Melvin, the florist,
for Jordan's wedding.

Jordan's wedding. The plans would proceed, full
steam ahead, with or without a bride. She felt as if she
had hopped on a runaway train headed straight on a
collision course. Would she be able to pull herself from
the rubble afterward or would she be buried alive?
Could she bear to watch him walk down the aisle with
another woman, knowing that she could have been his
bride? It would have taken only one simple word to
change her fate.

Yes. Yes, Jordan, I will marry you. Even though you
don't love me. Even though this marriage means no
more to you than a simple business deal.

Elise groaned and rubbed her eyes again, then ran her
fingers through her hair, brushing the strawberry-blond
strands away from her face. She had made the right decision. Jordan was not the man for her.

"Hello, dear."

Elise looked up as an older woman stopped before her
table. She tried to place the face, then realized it was the
woman she had met in Jordan's office. She was bun-

dled from top to toe in a pale-pink wool coat with a pink muffler wrapped around her neck and a jaunty tam of the same color perched on top of her head. She had on the same high-top sneakers that she'd worn the night Elise had met her. Her cheeks were rosy and her eyes twinkled merrily.

"Hello," Elise said warily. "How are you?"

"Why, I'm quite well. Thank you for asking. May I sit down?" Not waiting for an answer, she slid into an empty chair across the table and folded her gloved hands in front of her, staring sharply at Elise. "You don't look well at all. Is something wrong?"

Elise opened her mouth to speak, then snapped it shut. Who was this woman? Normally Elise would be offended by such blatant nosiness from a virtual stranger. But after a terrible night of tossing and turning, she found the woman's concern somehow comforting.

"It's Jordan, isn't it?" the woman continued.

Elise contained her look of surprise. "I—I don't believe we've ever been introduced. I'm Elise Sinclair."

The woman laughed and shook her finger playfully at Elise. "I knew that. Don't you remember, we met in Jordan's office? I never forget a face, or the name that goes with it."

"Of course I remember. But I'm afraid I don't recall your name."

"Well, maybe that's because I never told you."

She felt a sliver of irritation at the woman's deliberately evasive answer, but it dissolved in the face of her warm smile. "Who are you?" Elise asked bluntly.

The woman gazed out the window, intent on the hustle and bustle below, her words soft and direct. "The important question really is 'Who are you?'—isn't it?"

Elise calmly placed her coffee cup back in its saucer. "What's that supposed to mean?"

"Are you the woman who can teach Jordan to love again? Or are you like the other women in his life, interested only in his money, his position." She fixed Elise with a probing stare. "He asked you to marry him, didn't he?"

This time Elise knew her expression was one of shock. "How did you know that? Did Jordan talk to you?"

"Jordan is very secretive about his personal life. I think that has to do with his childhood. Did you know that his mother left him and his father when he was nine? Just up and walked out on them one day. No, I suppose he wouldn't have told you that. He loved his mother very much, though he'd never admit it. He tried so hard to maintain that stiff Prentiss upper lip." The old woman sighed, a faraway look in her eyes. "She died a year later in a car accident. Very tragic. I believe that's why Jordan has such a difficult time trusting his feelings."

Elise felt her heart twist in compassion for him. "You knew Jordan when he was a little boy?"

"Oh, yes. I knew him quite well."

Elise shook her head in bewilderment. "And you know about Edward and his attempt to take over BabyLove?"

"Of course I do," she replied, then laughed lightly, a lovely bell-like sound. "I can just imagine Jordan's proposal."

Elise couldn't help but smile. "It was a little bit odd. He listed all the things he could give me—cars, clothes, money. He's pretty desperate to save his company."

"Hmm." She nodded. "That's good. I knew he would feel that way. Now, I know this is probably none of my business, Elise. And I do make it a practice never to interfere in other people's lives. But I feel compelled to give you one little piece of advice. Don't be concerned about what he says he can give you. Be more concerned with what you can give him. The rest will come, I promise you."

The woman glanced at her watch and then stood up suddenly, her hands aflutter. "Well, there it is. I've said what I have to say and now I'll leave you to your coffee." She reached out and patted Elise's hand, then turned for the door. "Don't you worry," she called back over her shoulder. "Everything will turn out just fine. You'll make a lovely bride."

"Wait," Elise cried. "Come back here. You don't understand. I turned him down." Elise fumbled for her purse and tossed some money on the table. She pulled on her coat as she hurried out the door, trying to keep her eyes on the pink-clad form a hundred feet in front of her.

Whoever this woman was, Elise was determined to find out how she knew so much about Jordan Prentiss. She had to be a relative. Or at least a close family friend. Either way, she was privy to Jordan's marriage plans.

Elise kept the bobbing pink tam in sight as she followed her down the escalators, gaining on her until she was only fifteen feet behind her. Then the woman stepped into the revolving doors leading out to the street. Elise waited behind several other shoppers before she passed through the spinning door. She scanned the sidewalk for the woman in pink, but her frantic search revealed only drably attired shoppers and conservatively dressed business people, their heads bent to the wind, their eyes fixed on the sidewalk.

The old woman had vanished as she had appeared, only staying long enough to pass out a bit of grandmotherly advice. Elise stood outside the Bloomingdale's building for a full five minutes, searching the crowd, before she gave up and went back inside.

6

"'WEALTHY CHICAGO businessman, SWM, 38, seeks corporate wife, SWF, 25-35. Impeccable manners, good breeding, college degree and a practical approach to marriage required. Send list of qualifications ASAP to Box 13707, Chicago, Illinois.'"

"A singles ad?" Jordan asked. "You want me to run a singles ad?"

Pete Stockton nodded. "Just as a backup. Listen, boss, we're running a little short on time here. We've got to consider all the options at our disposal. Did you look at the files on the latest list of candidates yet? Maybe you could take them home tonight and review them, then make a few appoint—er, I mean dates—for this weekend."

Jordan glanced over at the stack of manila folders on the corner of his desk. He had been avoiding the task for two days, but he knew he could put it off no longer. Pete was right. Time was running out and he was no closer to finding a bride than he had been a month ago. "I'll go through them tomorrow. I've got plans for this evening."

Pete gave him an exasperated look. "I get the feeling you're having second thoughts about this, Jordan. Are you sure you still want to proceed?"

"I have no choice," Jordan snapped. "The board is wavering in their support for Edward, but I'm not in the

clear yet. This marriage could turn the tide in our favor."

"According to my schedule, you should at least have
the list narrowed to a few candidates. You've got to
make a proposal soon, and have an alternate in case
your first candidate refuses."

"She already did," Jordan muttered, snatching a file
folder from the pile and flipping through it.

"What are you talking about?"

He threw the folder down on his desk and pushed
back his chair. "I've made one proposal and collected
one refusal already."

"Who?"

Jordan stood up and walked to the windows. "It
doesn't make any difference who she is. She said no."

He had gone over to Elise's house expecting as much,
but had decided to give his marriage proposal a shot.
He had figured his odds of an acceptance were least one
in three—good odds by business standards. But then
he had blown the execution, and the odds had plum-
meted to zero.

Other business deals had fallen through for him in the
past, yet none of them had disturbed him in such a severe way. Jordan hated to lose. And he had lost because of a lack of preparation on his part. Her refusal
made him angry and frustrated, feelings he had never
allowed to enter into his business dealings.

If only he had been able to make her see his reasoning and the advantages to his plan. But her decision was
based on emotion rather than reason and he knew from
experience that when a business decision was made
with the heart instead of the head, the results were unpredictable at best. In this case, there was no use beat-

ing a dead deal. There wasn't a chance in a million that she would change her mind.

He'd tried to convince himself that it didn't matter...but it did. He could still feel the harsh sting of her refusal. But that was the downside. This crash and burn had an upside. He hadn't lost everything. Like the shrewd businessman that he was, he had taken his loss and turned it around, finding a way to salvage something from the wreckage. Elise had said his proposal was less than romantic and he knew she was right; the trouble was, he had no idea what she really meant by romantic. But after tonight's romance consultation he *would* know and he wouldn't make the same mistake twice.

"Just no? Didn't she give any reasons?" Pete persisted. "Did you try to change her mind? Was it a definite no or an ask-me-another-time no? Did she throw you out on your ear and tell you never to darken her door again? Or did she leave the door open a crack?"

"What the hell are you talking about?"

"How did she say no?"

Jordan shrugged. "I don't remember. All I remember was her answer and no means no."

"In most cases, I'd agree. But in the case of a marriage proposal, there might be room for negotiation. If you still want this woman, you shouldn't give up so easily."

Jordan turned and stared skeptically at his assistant. "What are you saying? You think I could change her mind?"

"It's worth a try. Right now, we don't have a better deal on the table. But I think you'd stand a better chance if you listened to a little advice."

Jordan laughed. Why was it everyone felt compelled to give him advice on romance? Did he have "bumbling idiot" tattooed across his forehead? "Since when did you become an expert in the field of marriage proposals? The last time I checked, you were a terminal bachelor."

"I don't claim to be an expert. I do, however, know how a woman likes to be treated. Just let me give you a few general pointers. What could it hurt? The worst she could do is say no again."

Jordan sat back down and kicked his feet up on the edge of the desk, then clasped his hands behind his head. Maybe Pete was right. What *did* he have to lose? In reality, he had an incredible amount to gain if Pete could help him: Elise, a wife and his company. He had already managed to make a mess of things on his own. Right now, he was willing to try anything. "All right, Stockton, fire away."

Pete clapped his hands enthusiastically. "Okay. First, a woman likes a man to be a man."

"I think I've got that one covered," Jordan replied dryly.

"I mean they really go for the rugged man—blue jeans, flannel shirts, cowboy boots. Three women . . ." Stockton shook his head in disgust. "*Three women* dumped me for blue-collar types. For some reason, women are attracted to the strong, silent, brooding guys. Lose the suit and tie and get yourself some blue jeans. And practice your brooding."

"Brooding?"

"Yeah," Stockton answered. "Sort of like this."

Jordan's assistant furrowed his brow, narrowed his eyes and clenched his teeth. To Jordan's eye, he looked as if he had just contracted a severe case of constipation.

"It makes a man seem mysterious. Women eat that stuff up. Mystery is a big turn-on."

"I'll remember that," Jordan replied. "Anything else?"

"Never, ever be late. For anything. It's like throwing a match on gasoline. I think it's something hormonal. It doesn't matter where you were or why you're late. I was late picking up Andrea, the woman I was dating before Jennifer, and she refused to let me in. I never saw her after that night."

"How late were you?"

"Three days. But that's beside the point. They live—and you die—by the clock."

"And what if I *am* unavoidably late?"

"Bring a gift. They're suckers for presents and it will give you a perfect excuse for being late—you were shopping. When I was dating Lisa, I kept a supply of gifts in the trunk of my car. In fact, if you really want to impress a woman, bring her something every time you see her. And something for her family, too. It never hurts to butter up the relatives. You may need them in your corner someday."

"What kind of presents would you suggest?"

"It doesn't matter, as long as they're expensive. Women go for those kitchen gadgets—you know, coffee makers and blenders. They like jewelry and clothes more, but those kind of presents are too risky in my opinion. You may get something she doesn't like and then you're in trouble because you didn't know she wouldn't like it. With an electrical appliance, you can't go wrong. What's not to like about a food processor?"

"A food processor." Jordan considered this information carefully, trying to remember what Elise had told him about gifts. Don't buy generic jewels, she had said. Buy her something that reminds you of her. Somehow a food processor was the last thing that came to mind when he thought of Elise. But maybe, if she liked to cook, it did make sense.

"And compliment her a lot. On her dress, her hair, her cooking. It makes no difference, just be profuse and sound sincere. Tell her she smells good, like a spring rain or a tropical breeze."

Jordan shot him a doubting look.

Pete waved him off. "I know, I know. It sounds stupid, but I use that one all the time and it works like a charm. Finally, be assertive. Don't ask her to marry you, tell her. Women like men who take charge. Sensitivity in our gender is highly overrated. Sweep a woman off her feet, like on the covers of those romance novels they're always reading. Don't be a wimp."

"Don't be a wimp," Jordan repeated.

"Show her who's boss. Be a man, a stud, a go-to guy."

"A go-to guy."

"Right," Pete urged.

"Right."

JORDAN PUSHED Elise's doorbell, then glanced down at his watch. Though he was twenty minutes early, at least he wasn't late. Usually he made it a practice to be punctual, always arriving at the agreed-upon time. He had thought about waiting in the car for a few minutes, but if women hated men who were late, they would probably love a man who was early. He would just tell Elise that he couldn't wait another minute to see her. This romance business really wasn't so difficult, after all.

Until his discussion with Pete that afternoon, he hadn't realized how little he really knew about pleasing a woman. He had always considered women an entirely different species, wonderfully satisfying in bed, but totally foreign to his mind. He had never taken the time to care about what they liked or disliked. His relationships with the opposite sex had never progressed far enough to make that data imperative.

But he was in the driver's seat now. Pete's insights were helpful, but Elise was about to provide him with everything he needed to turn the situation to his advantage. Though she wouldn't know it, she was about to hop on the Prentiss express, headed straight to the altar. Elise's lessons in romance were about to be put to work on the teacher herself. How could he go wrong? With a concentrated effort, he would have a confirmed deal with Elise Sinclair in a matter of days.

Jordan shifted the packages in his arms and rang the bell again. A moment later, the front door swung open to reveal Elise, her face flushed and moist, her hair wet and puddles of water forming at her feet beneath the hem of her shapeless bathrobe.

She looked at him in annoyance, then turned to the huge grandfather clock in the foyer. Slowly she returned her gaze to him. "You're early," she said. "I told you six o'clock. It's five-thirty. You got me out of the shower."

"Five-thirty-eight," Jordan corrected.

She arched her brow and stepped aside to allow him to enter. "You're still early."

"Sorry," he muttered. "I was anxious to get started." He followed Elise into the parlor, his eyes fixed on the provocative sway of her hips beneath the bulky bathrobe. What he wouldn't give to be able to pull the tie loose, push the robe off her body and explore the hidden curves beneath.

She turned to him and casually surveyed his appearance as she spoke, her expression showing mild surprise. "All right, let's start here and now. Never be early. It makes you appear too eager. Women want a man, not a lap dog. If you can't be on time, then be a little late." She ran her eyes down his length again. "Women expect that. Men are incapable of arriving on time and women factor that into their schedules. I expected you . . . to arrive at—what are you wearing?"

Jordan followed her gaze from his leather bomber jacket and flannel shirt, past his prewashed jeans to his feet. The pointed toes of his brand-new cowboy boots gleamed in the soft light of the parlor. "You like them, don't you?" he said as he held out his foot.

She shook her head and studied his footwear. "I'd be careful with those boots, Tex," she murmured. "You could put a person's eye out." Drawing a sharp breath, she pulled the belt of her robe tighter and nodded toward the couch. "Sit down. I'll be back in a few seconds."

He placed his packages on the coffee table and sat down, then pulled off the leather jacket and tossed it beside his gifts. So far, Pete was zero for two. He closed his eyes and leaned back, sinking into the soft depths of the couch. She didn't like men who were too prompt and she wasn't hot for the cowboy type. Stifling a groan, Jordan pushed himself off the couch and wandered restlessly around the room, picking up Elise's possessions, searching for a clue to her likes and dislikes.

She liked small objects. Nearly everything he picked up fit in the palm of his hand: a marble egg, an inlaid box, a delicate porcelain chickadee. And she liked flowers. Every surface was decorated with some type of floral design. Silk flowers spilled from vases and bowls scattered about the room. And a subtle floral scent wafted through the house. From what he could tell, her favorite color was either pink or green. He carefully filed the facts in his mind, then realized how trivial the information was.

Jordan walked to the fireplace and stared down into the cold ashes on the grate. What did he *really* know about her? He didn't know her favorite foods or what type of music she liked. He didn't know anything about her family or her childhood. All he knew of Elise Sinclair was the softness of her lips and the musical sound of her voice. He knew the exact color of her hair in sunlight and the way she bit her bottom lip when she was nervous. But she had revealed little solid information about herself in their business dealings. How the hell was he supposed to make this work?

He felt a soft nudge against his leg and looked down to find Elise's cats at his feet. Their tails switched back and forth on the Oriental carpet and their attention was transfixed by the shiny metal toes of his cowboy boots. He wiggled his foot and the white cat pounced, trapping his toe beneath its paws.

"At least there are a few females left in the world who find macho irresistible," he murmured, bending down to playfully poke at the furry feline. "You are ladies, aren't you?"

The gray cat approached, pushing her head beneath Jordan's hand before rolling over on her back. "You live with her," he whispered. "Maybe you could put in a good word for me. I'll make it worth your while. A lifetime supply of fresh tuna and catnip." The cats stared at him with vacant looks.

Jordan gave each cat an affectionate pat, then continued his survey of the room. As he passed the mirror above the mantel, he met his reflection with a critical glare. Stockton had spent a ridiculous amount on the clothes he wore and Elise hadn't been impressed. To tell the truth, Jordan hadn't been impressed, either, but his assistant had been adamant.

Maybe it was all in the attitude. Clothes, after all, didn't make the man. Jordan furrowed his brow. He narrowed his eyes and clenched his teeth trying to replicate his assistant's version of brooding.

"Are you all right?" Elise's reflection appeared in the mirror beside his, her face etched with concern.

Jordan quickly cloaked his contorted features with a bland smile. "Me? Yes. I'm fine." He turned to Elise, his gaze locking with hers. She shifted uncomfortably, running her fingers through the damp tendrils of her hair. "What about you? Are you all right?"

"What? With these lessons?" Elise asked. She shrugged. "Sure. As long as we keep this on a professional level. You need a wife in a hurry. It's as simple as that. I'll do what I can to help you." She raised her gaze to meet his.

"Good," he murmured. He stared into her liquid green eyes, unable to break a connection that suddenly crackled like a high-tension wire between them. An uncontrollable surge of desire washed over him and he felt his body draw closer to hers. His hand moved of its own volition, coming to rest on her silken check. Slowly he lowered his head to kiss her.

He brushed his lips gently across hers. When hers parted slightly to protest, he took advantage and covered her mouth to slowly sample her moist warmth with his tongue. To his surprise, she allowed him to continue his tender assault and he deepened the kiss, the wave of heat in his body now a raging tide.

Gradually, through his hazy passion, he realized that she wasn't responding. Her hands rested limply at her sides and her body stood unmoving before him, a pillar of reticence. He dragged himself from the drugging effects of the kiss and looked down at her. She opened her eyes and stepped away.

"That was very... nice," she murmured.

"Very nice," Jordan breathed, sliding his hands along her arms to her waist, drawing her to him again. And very romantic, if he did say so himself.

"Except..." she began.

"Except?"

"Well, this is just a suggestion, but you may want to... to impose a bit more... self-control. A kiss of greeting should be a bit less... less passionate. Less... wet."

Jordan froze. "What?"

"Not what. Wet," she said with emphasis. "Though it was, on the whole, a very romantic kiss. On a scale of one to ten, I'd give it a seven. Or maybe you'd prefer letter grades. That would be about a B-minus."

"You're grading me?"

"That's what you're here for, isn't it? Lessons in romance. I think it's best if we grade your efforts. That way, we can judge your progress."

Jordan glared at her, unable to speak, his temper threatening to explode. What kind of game was she playing? Her expression was cool, composed, as if she had suffered no effects from the dizzying kiss. He was tempted to yank her into his arms and give her an A-plus for effort, but instead he turned away and stalked to the couch.

So this was the way it was going to be. She was going to keep him at arm's length. He considered it a silent challenge—love her or leave her alone. He would play along. But Elise Sinclair had no idea what she was up against. Jordan never backed down from a challenge.

He had one advantage. She wanted him as much as he wanted her; he could see it in her eyes. He would have Elise Sinclair as his bride and without any admissions of undying love and eternal fidelity from him. Nothing would stand in his way.

Grabbing the largest gift-wrapped package from the coffee table, he turned and held it out to her. "Here, I brought you a present," he said smoothly.

Elise stepped toward him and took the brightly wrapped package from his hands with a winsome smile. "This is for me?"

Jordan watched her coolly. Two could play at this game. "No. It's for my future fiancée. I just thought I'd try it out on you first. You know, so you can grade me on it." She looked up at him and he shot her a tight grin. "Go ahead—open it."

Elise gave him a sideways glance as she tore into the paper. When the gift was unwrapped, she held the big box up in front of her and surveyed it with a confused look. "An ice-cream maker?"

Jordan nodded. In the store it had seemed like a brilliant idea. The saleswoman had gone on and on about the convenience of this particular model and the taste of homemade ice cream. And ice cream did remind him of Elise, sweet and delicious, smooth and creamy, cool, yet able to melt to his touch. And it fit Pete Stockton's suggestion of a small electric appliance.

"How . . . original," she said hesitantly. "Very unexpected."

"Unexpected is good. You told me that once."

"Yes, but usually one would buy a more personal gift for his future bride. But an ice-cream maker is very . . . original." She placed the box on the coffee table and picked up the remaining package. "What's this?"

Jordan tried to grab it out of her hand. "That's nothing."

"I'll be the judge of that." She pulled off the ribbon and foil paper, then lifted the lid from the smaller box. Digging through the tissue paper, she withdrew a tiny leather mouse. The confused look she had given the ice-cream maker was replaced by utter bewilderment. Then she withdrew a plastic ball with a bell inside, a miniature punching bag and a stuffed bird on an elastic string. "These are . . . cat toys."

"I know," Jordan answered defensively. "They're not for you—or my fiancée," he quickly added. "They're for your cats."

"You brought Clorinda and Thisbe presents?"

Jordan shrugged. "Sure. Why not?" They were the closest thing Elise had to a family. He didn't have much to work with, so he worked with what he had.

Elise frowned and opened her mouth, then snapped it shut, smiling at him, instead. "Thank you. It was a very thoughtful gift. I'm sure they'll enjoy these." She paused as if uncertain how to proceed, then took a deep breath. "Why don't we get started?"

"I thought we already had," Jordan said under his breath.

She sat down on the couch and looked up at him, waiting for him to join her. He sat down at the opposite end and watched her closely.

"All right," he prompted. "What do you have planned?"

"Close your eyes," she ordered.

After a brief questioning look, he complied.

"Now, describe what I'm wearing. No, don't look. Close your eyes. Tell me what I'm wearing."

Jordan concentrated hard, trying to bring up an image of Elise's clothing, but he drew only a blank. The problem was, from the moment she'd walked into the room, he had been captivated by the exquisite features of her face, the emerald depths of her eyes and the lush curve of her mouth. Hell, he had no idea what she was wearing. The only thing he knew was that right this minute, he wished she weren't wearing anything at all.

"Are you wearing a sweater?" he asked.

"Am I?"

"Yes, you're wearing a blue sweater," he said with more confidence.

"What shade?"

"I don't know," Jordan muttered. "Light blue, sky blue."

He opened his eyes to see if he was right, but she quickly placed her palm over them. "Keep them closed," she warned.

"So, was I right?"

"I'm wearing a white blouse with a green-and-black tapestry vest. It's important to be observant. You need to remember the little details of your relationship. It will help you be more romantic."

Jordan groaned in frustration. "Why don't you ask me something I know?" he protested in an angry voice. "Ask me about how your eyes sparkle when you smile or how your hair shimmers like spun gold in the sunlight. Ask me about how your mouth feels beneath mine or how your skin is like satin under my fingertips. Ask me—" Jordan snapped his eyes open just as she snatched her hand away from his brow, suddenly aware of what he was saying.

Elise watched him, wide-eyed, her lips parted and her breath coming in shallow gasps.

"Ask me something I know," Jordan repeated, his gaze penetrating hers.

Elise stood up and walked across the room to stand at an ornate lowboy, where she picked up a tiny vase filled with a spray of silk flowers. "That was very romantic," she said in a soft voice, plucking at the flowers nervously.

"So does it deserve a ten, or was it worth just a seven or eight?" he asked in a calculating voice, his earlier anger resurfacing at her swift retreat.

She spun around to look at him, her eyes registering a flash of hurt before she buried it beneath a blank facade. Jordan was startled. Had he really said something romantic? Had his words actually affected her?

"Jordan, I really don't think this is such a good idea, these lessons."

"Why not, Elise?"

"Because, I...it's just that you..." She sighed. "I can't help you be something you aren't. No matter how hard you try, some frogs just don't have prince potential."

Jordan stood and walked over to her. "Is that what you want, Elise? Some real-life Romeo who'll speak all sorts of flowery gibberish and kiss your feet."

"You know what I want. I want a man who loves me. A man I can depend on. A man who needs me."

"You want a lap dog, Elise, and life with a lap dog can be very dull."

"Well, maybe it will be, but at least I'll know where I stand."

"What about me?" He grabbed her by the arm and drew her against his chest. "*I need you*, Elise."

She twisted in his arms. "You don't need me, Jordan. You need a body, someone to wear a wedding dress in return for a generous salary. I already have a job. I don't need another."

"That's not the only thing I'm offering. I can give you more."

She met his gaze. "What can you possibly give me that I really want?" she asked.

"I can give you this." In a swift, sure movement, Jordan captured her mouth, moving his lips against hers in an erotic dance of sensation. His tongue traced her lower lip, then plunged into the warm recesses of her mouth.

With a weak shove, she pushed away and glared at him defiantly. "Three," she uttered, her eyes blazing with anger.

He dropped his mouth to hers again, this time plundering with greater force, sliding his hands along her spine until he cupped her buttocks. With gentle pressure, he pressed her hips into his. He suppressed a groan, skimming his mouth along the curve of her throat, his lips coming to rest over a thrumming pulse point. He bit her neck softly and she gasped.

"Five," she murmured, her voice shaky.

"Tell the truth, Elise. Are you willing to give this up just for some pretty words?" He pressed his hips into hers, his arousal an unyielding ridge of heat against her belly. He wanted her to feel the extent of his desire—the driving, uncontrolled inferno of passion that spread from deep inside him like a wildfire. But her next words doused the fire as quickly as a cold summer downpour.

"Yes," she croaked. "I'm willing to give all this up."

Jordan gazed down at her, meeting her arctic stare. A tear glimmered in the corner of her eye and a rush of self-contempt washed over him.

"Dammit, Elise. I know you want me. Don't try to deny it."

"I don't deny it," she replied, her voice barely above a whisper. "But it's not enough. I'm sorry, Jordan, but I can't play by your rules. They just don't work for me." She stepped to the coffee table and picked up his jacket, holding it out to him. "That's the way it is. I can't change the way I feel any more than you can change the way you don't feel."

"And what if you never find your perfect man, Elise?"

She shook her head. "That's a risk I have to take. I grew up with parents who were more in love with each other every day they were together. When my mother died, my father almost died from grief. A few years ago, he remarried. I think he was hoping to find the same kind of love he had with my mother, but it just wasn't there. He's happy, but it isn't the same. It's second best. I don't want to settle for second best. I want the whole thing."

"My parents married for love," Jordan recalled, his voice steeped in bitterness. "At least, that's what they thought. Then my father needed to devote more time to the business and my mother started looking for . . . diversions. She fell in love with the tennis pro at their country club and ran off with him. Don't you see, Elise? I need a woman who understands the demands on my time, a woman who won't go looking for diversions. Someone I can trust to be there when I need her, someone who won't be ruled by her emotions."

"So you've ruled out love completely. Just because it didn't work out between your parents isn't enough reason to renounce commitment entirely. What would life be without love?"

"A hell of a lot simpler."

Elise shook her head in resignation. "Somewhere out there is a woman who's a perfect fit for you, a woman who shares your bleak opinions. You have to find her, Jordan. I'm not that woman, and I never can be."

Jordan felt a sharp pain in his chest at her words. He wasn't ready to let her go yet. "I can't find her without your help."

"Yes, you can. You can be a very romantic man when you put your mind to it. You don't need my help to find a wife. Anyway, I think it would be best for both of us if we didn't see each other again until the wedding."

Suddenly he didn't care about anything but keeping Elise close to him. She was the one he wanted. No one else would do. An odd mixture of fear and desperation grew in the pit of his stomach, weighing his words down like a rock in a rushing river. "What about the wedding plans?"

"Most of the plans are in place. We can accomplish everything else over the phone."

"No," Jordan said. "This wedding is very important. I want to at least have a weekly status meeting. And we can combine the meeting with a romance lesson. We'll just meet at my office or in public."

Elise regarded him suspiciously. "Jordan, that's really not necessary. Everything is well under control. And I don't think romance lessons are going to help. Not if you don't believe in what's behind the romance."

"If I say it's necessary, it's necessary. I have a lot riding on this plan."

She sighed, then closed her eyes for a moment. When she opened them again, Jordan saw a new determination in their green depths. "All right, we'll meet once a week. And we will keep it strictly business."

Jordan nodded. Of course he would keep it strictly business. And his most important business at the moment was convincing Elise to marry him. "Strictly business," he replied. "I promise."

ELISE CLOSED the door behind Jordan, then leaned back against it. Tears threatened to spill from her eyes, but she controlled the urge to cry with a steely resolve. She had made her decision and now she would have to abide by it. No matter how attracted she was to Jordan Prentiss, he was not in love with her. And she could not consider marriage to him.

Yet she couldn't tolerate the thought of him marrying someone else. If only he didn't have this ridiculous deadline, maybe there would be a chance for them. But without time, she had no hope of making him fall in love with her. The deck had been stacked against them from the start. It just wasn't meant to be.

She had hoped her lessons in romance would put their doomed relationship into perspective, but she hadn't counted on the intensity of her feelings for Jordan. It wasn't easy to put them aside, to ignore the rush of desire she felt whenever he looked at her, the shiver of passion she felt at his mere touch. He was everything she wanted and everything she didn't want, all wrapped up in one.

But he didn't want *her*; he wanted a wife.

Why couldn't she put him out of her life once and for all? She would still be faced with meeting him once a week until this silly charade of a wedding was over. Why did she agree? Was she still clinging to the hope that he might fall in love with her?

The ring of the phone interrupted her melancholy thoughts. Elise picked up the receiver and uttered a halfhearted "Hello."

"Lizzie, is that you?"

The sound of her father's voice calling her by her childhood nickname brought another surge of tears to her eyes. "Hi, Daddy. Yes, it's me."

"You sound upset. Is everything all right?"

"Everything is…just fine." Elise drew a deep breath. "Just fine."

"It's eighty degrees here today. What's the temperature in Chicago?"

"It's cold," Elise said softly. "Very cold."

"Did you get the boiler fixed yet? Make sure you call Max Constanza to get an estimate. And while he's there have him take a look at that leaky drainpipe in the upstairs tub."

"Yes, Daddy. I will." Even from a thousand miles away, her father was still as protective as ever. During the past five years they had switched roles again. As a small child her father had been her hero, riding to her rescue at every scraped knee and terrifying nightmare. After her mother had died, Elise had been fiercely protective of him, trying desperately to make life easy for him. But around the time he'd met Dorthi, their roles had once again shifted back to a traditional hero-daughter relationship.

"You have enough money, don't you? I can send you a check for the boiler repair if that's the problem."

"I have plenty of money, Daddy. I just got a terrific wedding to plan. The biggest and best ever." An image of Jordan's handsome face swam in her mind and she pushed it away, concentrating on her conversation with her father. He was going on about her financial situation and she listened distractedly, interjecting a "Yes, Daddy" or a "No, Daddy" where appropriate.

"Honey, Dorthi wants to say hello. Let me put her on."

Elise's attention snapped back to the phone conversation. "No, wait. Daddy?" There was silence on the other end of the line. "Daddy?"

"Hi, Elise. It's Dorthi. How are the girls?"

Elise stifled a groan of dismay. Why couldn't her father realize how uncomfortable these conversations with her stepmother were? It wasn't that she didn't care for Dorthi. Dorthi was a kind and generous woman who had never even tried to become a mother to Elise. Elise was grateful to her for bringing her father out of his long mourning. But it was hard to talk to the woman who had attempted to step into her mother's place in her father's life. Dorthi had settled for being second best when she'd married Martin Sinclair and the most Elise could feel for her was a small amount of pity.

She answered the standard questions about Clorinda and Thisbe, then listened to her stepmother chatter on about the weather and their golf games, before she heard her father's voice on the line again.

"Are you sure you're all right, Elise? Dorthi says you sound a little down."

"I'm fine." She paused, then impulsively gave voice to a question that had plagued her from the day her father had remarried. "Daddy, would you answer a question for me and answer it truthfully?"

"If I can, Lizzie."

"Why did you marry Dorthi if you didn't love her?"

"Elise, what kind of question is that?" Her father sounded shocked. "Whatever gave you the notion that I don't love Dorthi?"

"I know you don't love her the way you loved Mother."

"But that doesn't mean I don't love her at all. Elise, love can come in many different ways. The love your mother and I shared was very special. And my love for Dorthi is just as special."

"But you never kiss her or hold her hand like you did with Mother. There's no romance between you."

"Romance isn't the most important part of love. There's respect and security. And a deep friendship and commitment. Maybe we didn't exactly love each other at first, but we were great friends. I needed her and she needed me. And I grew to love her more and more every day."

The phone line was silent for a long moment before her father spoke again. "Lizzie, what's wrong? Tell me where this is all coming from."

Elise was stunned by her father's admission. She was certain he hadn't loved Dorthi when they'd gotten married. But she had never considered that his feelings could have changed over the years.

I need you, Elise.

Jordan's words echoed in her mind. He needed her. But was that really enough to make a marriage work? They were attracted to each other; that much was clear.

And she did respect Jordan and considered him a friend. But would he, could he grow to love her as her father had grown to love Dorthi?

"Elise?"

"Daddy, I have to go now. I have an appointment and I'm late. I promise I'll call you in a few days... Yes, I love you too... Yes, I'll call Max Constanza. 'Bye, 'bye." Elise hung up the phone and placed it on the floor beside the couch. She flopped down on the chintz cushion and pulled a pillow over her face, pressing her hands to her ears and squeezing her eyes shut.

"I need you, Elise."

His words were joined by a second voice.

"Don't be concerned about what he says he can give you. Be more concerned with what you can give him. The rest will come, I promise you."

Would love really come later? Could she afford to take such a risk?

7

"GO AHEAD," Elise urged. "Just walk in and look around. When you see something interesting, take it to the counter and buy it."

Jordan glanced at the shop window, then back at Elise. "What if I don't see anything I like?"

Elise smiled. "You're a man. I can guarantee you'll find something you like."

"Do I have to do this?" he grumbled. "Don't they have mail-order catalogues for these kinds of things? Wouldn't it be much better—educationally, I mean—to be able to study the products and discuss this particular area of romance before I jump in?"

Elise's expression was unyielding. This was one argument he couldn't hope to win. He had asked for romance lessons and now he was getting them. He never thought he would so soon have cause to regret his ploy to stay close to Elise.

Jordan glanced up at the name of the shop: Unmentionables. Around him, the evening shoppers at Water Tower Place strolled past, oblivious to his plight. In front of him, a series of scantily clad mannequins, surrounded by baskets of colorful underwear, seemed to regard him with haughty eyes. And through the huge plate-glass window, he could see a number of women shoppers inside the store, but not a single male patron.

This shop was the fifth they had visited that evening and Jordan knew why Elise had saved it for last in her lesson on gift buying. He had breezed through the first store, choosing an exotic, flowery perfume. He didn't mention that the scent reminded him of her. She had approved of his choice, then hustled him off to their second stop, a jewelry store, where he chose a hand-crafted pin of silver and jade, shaped like a cat. That choice had won him the reward of a hesitant smile. A candy store was next and he bought a pound of gourmet jelly beans, the exact color of her eyes. When he explained his reasoning, an uncomfortable look swept across her face and she avoided his gaze.

Store number four was a bit of a challenge. The import gift store offered a wide selection and Jordan spent nearly thirty minutes looking for just the right gift, something unique, something that Elise would consider romantic. He left with an ornate gold filigree key nestled inside a velvet-lined rosewood box. Her first reaction to his choice was one of confusion. But then he explained that the key was very special. It was the key to his heart. He had been proud of that effort, but when Elise had quickly excused herself to find the ladies' room, he wondered if he had inadvertently made another blunder.

Staying close to Elise through these romance lessons should have made his job easier. He had already gained incredible insight into her romantic nature, information that he could now use to break down her resolve. Over time, he had hoped that she would finally give up her silly notions about love and marriage and realize that he would make a good choice for a husband. Unfortunately, he hadn't made much progress in a positive direction. She kept each consultation on a business level, never giving a clue to her real feelings.

Jordan knew she had understood the significance of his purchases. They weren't generic romantic gifts chosen for a phantom fiancée, but gifts chosen especially for her. Throughout the night he had searched her expression for some crack in her indifferent facade. He was certain the gold key would do it. But after she had returned from the ladies' room, she had simply complimented him on his choice and the sentiment, then hustled him off to the next stop—a lingerie store.

Jordan looked down at his watch and, to his dismay, found at least a half hour left before the stores closed. Shopping for perfume was one thing, but shopping for ladies' underwear was an entirely different matter. He would just have to walk in, choose a romantic gift as quickly as possible, and hope that whatever he returned with was acceptable. With an encouraging smile from Elise, he pushed open the glass doors and walked inside.

Feigning an careful air of nonchalance and prior experience, he strolled slowly through the shop, stopping now and then to examine a lacy item before moving on. At first the sexy underwear held no interest. But then he came upon an incredibly transparent black robe and he caught himself wondering what Elise might look like wrapped in the filmy gauze. He imagined her perfect breasts pushing out against the sheer fabric, the feel of her hardened nipples through the thin barrier. And lower still, the lush curve from her waist to her hip, the shadow of soft hair where her thighs met.

A wave of heat raced through his body and a telltale throbbing began just below his belt. Stifling a groan, Jordan spun away from the robe and scanned the store. A rack of plastic-wrapped packages caught his attention and he strode over to a display of ladies' silk stockings. He grabbed a package labeled Misty Midnight and hurried over to the counter. The saleslady smiled as he slapped down his credit card.

"Is this a gift?" she asked.

Startled by her interest, Jordan met her friendly gaze. "What?"

"Is this a gift?" she repeated. "Would you like a gift box?"

Is this a gift? What else would it be? She didn't believe he planned to wear these himself, did she?

"Ah . . . yes. A gift. Thank you."

"You know, we have some lovely garter belts on display. Maybe you'd like to take a look at those. Or, if you prefer, I can show you some of our Merry Widow ensembles."

"Garter belts?" Jordan asked.

"To hold up the stockings," she whispered.

Jordan leaned closer. "Just how many garter belts would one need to hold up these particular stockings?"

"Just one. Or you can buy a Merry Widow. That comes with garters and panties."

He shifted uncomfortably on his feet and glanced around the store. "A Merry Widow would be fine. Why don't you choose one for me."

"What size?"

Was there no end to this? Jordan wondered. He felt like he was under the Spanish Inquisition. If this was the price he had to pay for learning to be romantic, it wasn't worth it. "Ten," he blurted out. "And I'm not answering any more questions. Just ring the blasted thing up so I can get out of here."

The sales clerk scurried off to retrieve his selection and returned a few moments later with three of what he assumed were Merry Widows—rather revealing items of underwear—in black, red and white. He pointed to the black and within a minute he had exited the store, with his Merry-whatever tucked safely in a box.

He found Elise sitting on a bench outside the shop, picking through the bag of jelly beans. She smiled and stood as he approached. "See, that wasn't so bad, was it?"

"Compared to what? Ripping my clothes off and jumping naked into the Chicago River from the top of the Wrigley Building? Or taking a nap in the middle of Division Street during rush hour?"

"Jordan, lingerie can be a very romantic gift. I just thought it would be good for you to try your hand at shopping for it. What did you buy?"

She reached for the bag, but Jordan snatched it away and hid it behind his back. "Never mind."

"Come on," Elise teased. "You did so well on the other gifts. Let me see."

"No. I'll just have to accept an incomplete on this part of the lesson. Let's get out of here. I've had enough shopping for one night."

Jordan grabbed Elise's elbow and steered her toward the exit. When they reached the street, she stopped and pulled out of his grasp, their easy-going banter suddenly gone. "I'll just catch a cab home," she said in a cool voice.

Jordan bit back an irritated reply. This had become a regular ritual with them at the end of each lesson. A warm hug or a passionate kiss could have put a proper end to the evening. But as much as he wanted to wrap her in his arms, her prickly attitude invited no intimate contact between them. A handshake was the best he could expect.

Damn, he was running out of time. This plan to break down her resolve was quickly losing steam and he was no closer to changing her mind than he had been after her refusal. Why did she have to be so damn stubborn? Why couldn't she admit her desire for him? He knew they would be good together, knew that their marriage could work. But she was holding out for a declaration of love, something that he wasn't prepared to give her. He sighed inwardly. Maybe it was time to turn up the gas, to be more aggressive.

"I'll drive you," Jordan replied. "My car's parked at the office."

"That's really not necessary. I can find—"

"I'm driving you home, Elise. End of discussion."

Surprised by his tone, she nodded and they turned and walked briskly down Michigan Avenue.

"You did quite well tonight," she said, breaking the silence that had lasted a city block.

Jordan's irritation slowly dissolved at the soft, musical sound of her voice. "Thanks. It was fun."

She returned his smile. "Yes, it was."

Jordan yanked her to a stop, grabbed her shoulders and turned to her to him. "I always seem to have a good time when I'm with you, Elise. Why is that?"

She avoided his probing gaze, watching a pedestrian pass by instead. "Maybe it's because we're friends now. There's nothing between us but business and it makes it easier to relax, to be ourselves."

She looked up at him with wide green eyes, silently pleading for confirmation. Jordan smiled tightly and quelled an urge to argue the point. "Yeah, right," he said. "We're friends. That must be it."

The balance of the walk to Jordan's car and the ride home were spent in inane conversation about the

weather and Chicago politics. Jordan could tell Elise
had something else on her mind by the nervous set of
her smile. He pulled the Mercedes to the curb in front
of her house, shut off the engine, and waited for her to
speak.

She drew a deep breath. "How is your search for a
bride coming along?"

"Fine," Jordan replied.

"Does that mean you've found someone?"

"Not yet. But don't worry, I will. There's still time."

"I don't think we need to continue the romance lessons," she blurted out. "You've done very well and I
think it's time to...end them." She reached for the door
handle, but Jordan grabbed her arm to stop her.

"Elise, wait."

She looked down at his hand on her arm, her expression cold and distant. But this time he refused to
pull away. Instead Jordan reached up and brushed his
palm against her cheek. God, she was so soft, like warm
silk. Slowly his thumb traced the outline of her full
lower lip and he watched as her eyes widened in alarm.
A kaleidoscope of conflicting emotions glittered in their
emerald depths, but she didn't pull away. She opened
her mouth to protest, but he placed his thumb across
her lips, gently teasing and caressing the soft flesh.

Then he saw the signal he was waiting for. Desire
flickered across her expression and he moved to cradle
her face in his hands. His mouth came down upon hers
in a touch more intimate, more demanding, more satisfying than that of his fingers on her lips. She opened
to him and he deepened his kiss, drawing her closer,
absorbing the feel of her in his arms and inhaling her
sweet scent, tasting the tentative touch of her tongue
against his.

The urge to look at her, to assure himself of the longing he felt in her kiss, was overwhelming and he drew away. Was she finally ready to admit they belonged together? Had they finally broken through the insurmountable wall that seemed to separate them? His gaze locked with hers and they stared at each other for what seemed like an eternity, paralyzed by the passion that washed over them both. But then the guarded expression returned to her eyes and she spoke.

"I—I have to go in now," she said. Her voice was empty of emotion and his heart twisted in his chest. What would it take to get through to her? Why couldn't she see how much he cared? Reluctantly, he released her and watched as she moved to open the door.

Before she had a chance to step out of the car, he reached into the back seat, collected his purchases and pushed them at her. "Here, take these. I bought them for you."

She hesitated, as if she were going to refuse, then nodded and clutched the packages to her chest. He watched her hurry up the front walk and disappear inside the house. Then, in a flash of temper, he slammed his hands against the steering wheel and cursed.

The romance lessons were over. And now it was time to put a quick and painless end to this ridiculous search for a wife, as well.

JORDAN STOOD over Elise's shoulder, pretending interest in the huge book of wedding invitations that lay open on the conference table in his office. His attention was drawn, instead, to the soft curve of her neck. His fingers ached to touch her there, but he clenched his fists at his sides.

"What about this one?" Elise asked, her slender finger coming to rest on another alternative, which to his eyes looked no different from the last hundred they had considered.

"Nope." Jordan bent closer, inhaling the fragrant scent of her hair.

"This one?"

"No." His chin brushed against her hair and the intimate contact sent a jolt of heat pulsing to his lap.

"How about this one?"

"I don't think so." His breath teased at the soft strawberry-blond strands tucked behind her ear.

Elise slammed the book shut and stood up suddenly, unaware how close he was. Her shoulder collided with his chin, snapping his teeth together and sending him stumbling backward. She spun around to face him, backing up against the edge of his conference table and regarding him warily.

"We've looked at every book of wedding invitations in the city of Chicago. *You* were the one who wanted to be involved in this decision. I would appreciate it if you would make a choice sometime this century."

Jordan caught a glint of suspicion in her eyes. He wondered when she was going to catch on to his new stalling tactics. After the abrupt end to their romance consultations, Jordan had insisted on becoming involved in the most minute details of the wedding, disagreeing with every choice Elise made and demanding another set of options for every decision. Phone calls were not enough to cover all the information Jordan requested, so they had met first once a week, then twice and now three times a week. Jordan found the plan quite clever in its simplicity. The more involved he became in the wedding, the more time he got to spend with Elise. Unfortunately, each encounter left him craving her warm, willing body—and settling for a cold shower.

Elise, however, steadfastly maintained a chaste distance between them, as if their encounter after the shopping trip had only served to strengthen her determination. She was polite, if somewhat reserved, ignoring evidence of his desire for her, as she had done just moments ago.

The stress was taking its toll, though. Jordan could see the lines of tension that outlined her perfect features and the dark smudges beneath her eyes. She looked like she wasn't getting much more sleep than he was and that was precious little. With each meeting, he became a bit more aggressive in his pursuit, tempting her here and there with an innocent brush of his hand or a long, potent stare. If he could just wait her out, he was sure she'd give in.

"If you don't choose an invitation tonight, I'll do it for you," Elise threatened. "This is the last decision that needs to be made, so let's just get it over with. If I don't order the invitations this week, they won't be ready in time. The wedding is little more than a month away."

The last decision? Did that mean there would be no more reason for them to meet after tonight? Even through her reserved facade, he could tell Elise was close to capitulating. But without an excuse to be near her, the odds of getting her to agree to his marriage proposal were virtually nil. And without Elise, there would be no wedding. From the moment he had asked Elise to marry him, he hadn't made a single attempt to find another bride.

He had placed everything he cherished, his company and his future, on the line in the hopes that Elise would come around, that she would finally agree to marry him. And now, the whole mess was on the verge of falling apart.

If only control of BabyLove wasn't tied into the whole deal. Without the need to save his company, Jordan could wait forever for Elise. He could give her the time she needed to realize they belonged together. But the entire idea was really a moot point. He could never give up his company.

Or could he?

Jordan banished the ridiculous thought from his mind. BabyLove was his life, his future. And what was Elise? She was his— He swallowed a rush of denial at the words that came to mind. His happiness. No, she was a woman, he rationalized. A desirable, fascinating woman. A woman he wanted more than he had ever wanted anyone before. That was all.

Jordan stepped back to the conference table and casually flipped through the album of invitation samples. He paused over one page, then pointed to it. "This one," he ordered, his voice tight.

Elise turned to the table and nodded at his choice. "That's a very nice invitation."

She stood beside him for a long time, her posture stiff, her eyes fixed on the album. He bit back a hiss of frustration, then spun on his heel and walked over to his desk. Keeping his attention directed at her, he sank down onto his chair.

With a barely perceptible sigh, Elise sat down on one of his guest chairs. "What about the copy?" she asked, avoiding his glance with a concentrated study of his desk clock.

"I'll leave that up to you."

She hesitated before she spoke, then proceeded in a shaky voice. "I need the bride's name."

"As I said, I'll leave that up to you."

Her head snapped up and she looked at him with wide eyes. "You haven't found a bride yet? But I thought . . ."

Jordan shrugged. "I have five weeks. I didn't want to rush into a decision. Marry in haste, repent in leisure. Isn't that how the saying goes?"

"But the invitations . . ."

"Send them out without a name. Jordan Broderick Prentiss and his fiancée cordially invite you to their wedding. Short and to the point and certain to pique interest in attending. Who will Prentiss marry? Show up at the church and see." The last was said with more than a hint of sarcasm.

"I cannot send invitations out without the bride's name."

"There's a simple solution to the problem, Elise. Just put your name on the invitation."

"No."

Her answer was uttered without emotion, though it caused a rising flood of frustration in Jordan. In a blaze of anger, he grabbed a stack of file folders from a pile on his desk and tossed them in her direction. They scattered across the desk in front of her. She stared at the folders for a moment, before glancing up at him with a cautious look. "Go ahead," he challenged. "Take a look. I'll leave the decision up to you."

"What decision?"

"My bride. You choose and you'll have that name you need for the invitation."

With a contemptuous arch of her brow, Elise pulled a folder off the pile and flipped through the contents, lingering for a long while over the photograph. The defiance chiseled in the hard set of her mouth softened, then faded completely. "She's very beautiful," she said in a strangled voice.

Jordan shrugged. "They all are."

She took another folder from the pile and perused the papers within. "And well educated."

"Yes, very well educated."

She grabbed a third folder and examined Stockton's summary and the picture carefully. "From very prominent families, too."

"Of course. Only the best."

She sighed wearily and placed the folders back on his desk, fixing her eyes on her folded hands.

"So, who would you choose, Miss Sinclair? You've made so many fine choices in planning this wedding, certainly you could make just one more. Traci Van Slyke is a beauty. Jane Kirkpatrick holds a master's degree in architecture. And I'm sure you're aware of the benefits of marrying into Eileen Pomeroy's family."

"I—I think you should marry whichever woman you want."

Jordan shot to his feet and slammed his palms down on his desk. "And I think you know who I want to marry. Stop avoiding the question, Miss Sinclair. Who will it be? Who should I marry?"

Elise stood and placed her palms opposite his, leaning over the desk in a threatening posture that matched his own. The disinterested look in her eyes had been replaced by flaming anger and Jordan felt a sudden stab of relief. He still had the ability to draw her feelings to the surface. She still cared.

Her soft, heart-shaped mouth was drawn into a tight line and her voice was low and even. "I don't give a damn who you marry. I don't care if you marry Traci or Staci or the man in the moon. All I care about is getting this wedding over and done with." She snatched a pad of paper from his desk and grabbed a pen, then scribbled down a phone number and tossed the pad back at him. "When you've made a decision about the invitations, call the printer. You've got until Tuesday morning to give him a name. I'll pick the invitations up on Wednesday afternoon and send them out."

She pulled her coat from the back of a chair and tucked her briefcase under her arm. "It's been a pleasure doing business with you, Mr. Prentiss. I'll see you and your bride at the wedding."

She stalked out Jordan's office door and slammed it shut behind her.

ELISE PUNCHED at the down button for the elevator with her finger. When the doors didn't open immediately, she tapped it again and again, her frustration level at its breaking point. Glancing over at the lit panel of numbers beside the doors, she saw that none of the three elevators was near the twenty-third floor. Afraid that Jordan would follow her, she hurried to the fire-exit door, pushed it open and stepped into the brightly illuminated stairway.

Leaning over the railing, she looked down between the flights. The dizzying twenty-three-story drop caused her already nervous stomach to lurch. With a deep breath, she started down the stairs. As she rounded the landing for the twenty-first floor with her eyes fixed on her feet, she came to a sudden stop as she nearly ran into another person heading up the stairs. A cry of alarm burst from her lips and she frantically grabbed for the railing to save herself from tumbling down the next flight of stairs. She regained her balance by sitting down with a painful jolt on the edge of a concrete stair.

"Ouch!"

"Oh, my!" a familiar voice exclaimed. "Are you all right?"

Elise looked up to see a figure in high-top tennis shoes and a pink sweatsuit holding on to the railing on the other side of the stairwell. She closed her eyes and shook her head, but the woman was still there when she opened them again.

"Wha-what are you doing here?" Elise sputtered, trying to bring her racing heartbeat under control.

"I'm exercising," the woman answered brightly, plopping down beside her. "It's all the rage, this stair climbing. You should give it a whirl. Exercise would do you a world of good. You're looking a little stressed out, my dear."

"I nearly fell down twenty-one flights of stairs!" Elise gasped, rubbing her sore backside. "How am I supposed to look?"

"Don't be silly. I would have caught you. I'm quite strong, you know. I pump iron. Right now, I'm working on my biceps." She crooked her arm and clenched her fist. "Lars, my trainer, says my muscle definition is outstanding." She poked at her upper arm with her index finger and smiled. "Besides," she added distractedly, "it wouldn't do to have Jordan's intended breaking any bones a month before the wedding. Now tell me, how are your wedding plans coming?"

Elise stared at her openmouthed, then brought her elbows to her knees and buried her face in her hands, moaning softly. She felt as if she had just stepped into the Twilight Zone. Why was this crazy woman always appearing at the worst of times with her disturbing insights? And why was she so determined to encourage a marriage between Elise and Jordan?

"Plans for Mr. Prentiss's wedding are nearly complete," Elise mumbled through her fingers. "But I have no intention of walking down the aisle with the man."

The woman grabbed Elise's hands and gave them an affectionate squeeze. "Of course you'll marry Jordan."

"Don't say that! It's not true. It won't happen."

"You love him and he loves you."

"I do not—" Elise looked into her sparkling eyes. "He doesn't—" Tears threatened and she bit her lip, tipping her chin up in defiance.

"He does," the woman answered softly, patting her on the shoulder. "He doesn't know it yet, but Jordan is a clever boy. A bit thick at times, but one can't blame him for the traits he inherited from his grandfather, Jonathan. Lord, that man could be stubborn. That silly stock option plan is a perfect example. If he hadn't—" She stopped and smiled apologetically. "I do go on, don't I. Now, what were we talking about? Oh, yes, Jordan. He'll realize he loves you soon enough."

Elise gave her a morose look. "How can you be so sure?"

"Do you think I would waste all my efforts on a lost cause? You and Jordan belong together. It was meant to be. And on April 18, I plan to be there to watch you walk down the aisle to marry him. It's all very simple, Elise. Trust me."

"Trust you? How can I trust you? I don't even know your name. Who are you?"

"Why, my name is Esme. I thought I told you."

Elise swallowed, then stared at her. "No! I mean who *are* you?"

"I told you, dear. You must learn to listen more carefully. If not to me, then to your heart." Esme stood up and brushed off the seat of her sweatpants. "I really have to be going. I have a lot of work to do before your wedding."

"Work?"

She nodded. "If I expect to fit into my pink chiffon, I need to lose at least five pounds. Lars and I are going to work on my hips this week." She laughed. "Sounds deliciously sinful, doesn't it?"

"Wait a second. I have to ask you—"

Esme jogged up to the landing, then gave her a jaunty wave. "Can't stop for too long," she said. "Have to keep the heart rate up. Ta, ta."

"No, wait," Elise called. She slowly pulled herself to her feet, rubbing her sore backside again, then followed the woman. When she reached the next landing, the door to the hallway was just closing. Elise pushed it open and stepped into the hall, expecting to catch sight of Esme's pink jogging suit.

But the hall was eerily empty. She moved to the elevators and watched the lights beside the doors move from floor to floor. None of them was close to the twenty-second floor.

"Esme?" she called. The name echoed back at her from the glass-and-marble hallway. "Esme?"

Elise stood in the middle of the hallway, a frown of consternation on her brow. "Oh, Esme. What am I supposed to do? Can I really believe you?" She closed her eyes and tipped her head back, releasing a tightly held breath. "If only I could be as sure as you that Jordan would come to love me. What do you know that I don't? Tell me, Esme. Please tell me. What should I do?"

"Push the button," a voice replied.

"Push the button?" she whispered back. "I don't understand. What button?"

"The button by the door," the voice said.

Elise opened her eyes with a start. An elderly man in a business suit stood in front of her.

"If you want to go up, you push the button with the arrow going up," he explained. "To go down, push the other button."

Elise felt her face color as she gave the man a quick smile. "Th-thank you. I'll remember that," she murmured. "But I'm in a hurry. I think I'll take the stairs." She reached the stairwell door just as a bell signalled the elevator doors were opening. For a moment, she hesitated, her gaze darting between the man and the elevator doors. But in the end she turned and took the stairs down one floor, too embarrassed to spend the trip down with the curious man.

As she waited for the elevator one floor below, her thoughts drifted back to Esme's declaration.

"You love him and he loves you."

Esme was right on one count. Elise did love Jordan. She had loved him from the moment she'd met him. But could she trust Esme's instincts about Jordan loving her? Could she trust the word of a stranger to make the most important decision in her life?

THE LIGHT from the television screen cast a blue glow across Jordan's darkened living room. He lay sprawled across the leather couch, his suit jacket crumpled on the floor beside him, his tie unknotted. A crystal tumbler of scotch and melted ice rested on his chest. With an impatient curse, he held out the remote control and fast-forwarded through the old black-and-white movie he was watching.

Elise had given him a list of Cary Grant movies to watch after their second romance consultation, claiming that the actor was the epitome of a romantic man. He had sent Stockton out to rent the videos. Along with the Cary Grant movies, Pete had returned with his own recommendations, advising Jordan that in his book, Cary Grant was a wimp.

Jordan had enjoyed the action movies on Pete's list. The men were tough and resourceful, rarely wore a shirt and carried rather large firearms. They avoided numerous explosions with amazing aplomb and managed to beat almost every bad guy to a pitiful pulp. And they had women falling at their feet like trees at a lumber camp.

Jordan had studied the movies, trying to ascertain how these action heroes had attracted such beautiful, willing women. There were no pretty gifts, no romantic dinners, no words of affection and not a single "I love you." Somehow these guys managed to avoid romance at every turn, yet still got the girl.

Too bad life didn't imitate art. Why couldn't Elise be more like the women he'd seen in these movies? Why was she so intent on a profession of undying love? Maybe Cary Grant had the answer, he had thought.

But after patiently sitting through four Cary Grant movies, Jordan was no closer to an answer. Pete had been right. Cary Grant was a wimp, always giving in to the woman, admitting his eternal devotion.

Jordan picked up the last movie on Elise's list and studied the cover. *Indiscreet*. An appropriate title, he thought to himself. Maybe that's just how she thought of their relationship. A foolish encounter. A momentary lapse in propriety.

And maybe that's how he should begin to think of it. At this moment, he didn't hold out much hope for resolving their differences. Elise was stubbornly clinging to her ideals and would settle for nothing less that a total surrender on his part. And he had no intention of hoisting the white flag and giving in to emotion.

I love you. Three simple syllables. Three simple words packed with unfathomable meaning. Why couldn't he say them? Why couldn't he *feel* them? All he felt right now was utter emptiness and anger. And longing—incredible, aching desire for her. It wasn't love; it was lust, pure and simple. When he was with her, he felt complete somehow, as if she filled him with warmth and surrounded him with satisfaction and contentment. And when they were apart, he felt cold and alone and numb to any emotion.

I love you.

"I—I love you." He frowned. He couldn't remember ever saying that exact combination of words before. Somehow he had thought they would be difficult to say. "I love you," he repeated. The words came without hesitation. But they were only words, without meaning and detached from any recognizable emotion he felt.

Jordan tried to remember if he'd ever heard the words before. His parents had never said them to each other in his presence. And he was sure his father had never uttered the endearment to him. But somewhere, in the back of his mind, he could hear his mother's voice. She had loved him, once, a long time ago. But then she had left and never come back.

How easily love could be tossed aside to make room for something, or someone, else. And how easily the words came out. He wondered why Elise set such store by them when they seemed to mean so little.

Jordan shook his head, then gulped down the rest of the watered-down scotch. Who was he to philosophize about love? He had never truly been loved, nor had he ever loved another. He wasn't sure he'd recognize the venerable emotion if it fell out of the sky and dropped at his feet.

What difference did love really make anyway? He had all he wanted in life, he had BabyLove...at least for another month. And then what? What if he lost the company? Jordan waited for the familiar rush of desperation and fear to twist in his chest and shatter his composure. He waited, and it came, but not with as much vengeance as it had in the weeks past.

He could live through losing BabyLove. He'd do what his grandfather had done years ago. He would start another company. Jordan closed his eyes and shook his head. Why waste time pondering what would never happen? He wasn't about to let his company go.

He stared at the video cover. He may not recognize love, but he'd be damned if he couldn't figure out something as simple as romance. If Elise thought Cary Grant was romantic, then Jordan would find out why. Even if he had to watch every one of his ridiculous movies all over again.

TEARS COURSED down Elise's cheeks, their warm saltiness mixing with the taste of green jelly beans. Elise grabbed a tissue from the box beside her on the bed and wiped at her watery eyes, before putting another handful of candy in her mouth. *Indiscreet* played quietly on the VCR and she watched the final scenes of the

romantic comedy, reduced to mush by the perfectly
romantic storybook ending.

Why couldn't life be like the movies? With a frustrated moan, she tugged at her twisted bathrobe, trying to cover her bare chest and thighs. Sexy lingerie was
certainly not constructed for warmth, she thought to
herself. But, then again, there was usually a source of
warmth close by when dressed in a black Merry
Widow, bikini panties and silk stockings with a seam
running up the backs.

Just yesterday, Jordan's gifts were in the garbage. She
wanted no reminder of him and their ill-fated relationship. But Elise's romantic nature had gotten the better
of her, and she'd retrieved the gifts and hid them in her
closet. Curiosity and a good dose of melancholy got the
better of her and the empty boxes were now scattered
across her bedroom floor.

She picked up the perfume and pulled out the stop-
per, then inhaled the exotic Oriental scent. A hint of
jasmine drifted through the room as she dabbed a bit
more of the scent on her throat and at her pulse points.
The cat pin was fastened to her chenille bathrobe and
the half-empty bag of jelly beans sat on her bedside table along with the filigree key in the rosewood box.

She reached over and picked up the key. Jordan had
said it was the key to his heart. She smiled ruefully. If
only it were that simple. Just turn a key, flip a switch,
open a door, and Jordan would love her as much as she
loved him.

Elise sniffled then pressed the remote to rewind
through the final scene of the movie. The sophisticated
story of two lovers torn apart by misunderstandings
had always been a favorite of hers. Her affair with Jordan was much like that of the characters portrayed by

Cary Grant and Ingrid Bergman, she mused. A creative, loving woman falls in love with a playboy businessman. The hero admits he's married to another . . . Elise shoved another handful of jelly beans into her mouth and continued to stare at the screen. Well, Jordan wasn't really married to another—yet. But he had told her he was engaged when he really wasn't.

And even though Ingrid knows he's married, she agrees to a discreet affair with Cary. Elise frowned. All right. So their stories weren't exactly alike, but they were pretty darn close. When Ingrid finds out that Cary really isn't married, that he's lied to protect his comfortable bachelor status, she plots her revenge. And when Cary shows up at her apartment . . . Elise sighed. And when Cary shows up at her apartment, Ingrid's plans for revenge fly out the window and she falls into his arms. And of course, Cary professes his undying love for her.

Elise smoothed the bedspread across her legs and leaned back against the pillows propped against the headboard. So much for the fortitude of the 1950's movie heroine. Luckily, the nineties woman was much more determined. But even though Ingrid gave in to the passion, love did triumph in the end. Love always triumphs at the ends of movies, she countered silently. Too bad real life didn't live up to the fantasies created in Hollywood.

She had left Jordan at his office earlier that day, and already it seemed as if they had been apart for weeks. Elise had looked forward to each and every meeting they'd had, even though she'd had to pretend differently. Elise felt a brief surge of guilt. She had even made some incredibly tasteless decisions for the wedding just so he would disagree and ask for more choices.

The thought of not seeing him again until his wedding day was almost enough to start the tears rolling. And the thought of him waiting at the front of the church for another woman nearly caused another fit of weeping.

Elise blew her nose. Maybe there was still hope. He hadn't chosen a bride yet, though by the files he had thrown at her, he had plenty of choices. So why hadn't he made a decision? Could Esme be right about his feelings? Could he be in love without knowing it?

With a groan, she burrowed beneath the covers. How did things get so incredibly confusing? She felt as if she were being pulled in a million different directions. One part of her was madly in love with Jordan Prentiss. Another part was rational enough to realize that he was the exact opposite of what she had dreamed of for a husband. Her practical side argued that at least he was being honest with her and honesty was one aspect of a relationship that she held in almost as much esteem as love. Then there was her optimistic nature. She, imagined it might be possible that, given time, Jordan could fall as deeply in love with her as she had with him. He did have his good points—he was dependable, handsome, smart, loyal. And she had to admit that her romance lessons did have an effect on him. She could do much worse.

What guarantees were there, anyway? Could she be certain that she would find someone better, someone she loved as much as she loved Jordan? Even if she fell in love with someone else and he loved her, who could say what the future would hold? At least with Jordan, what she saw was what she got. She knew exactly where she stood.

Yes, Jordan, I will marry you. The words were almost too unthinkable to say.

Her lips parted, the words forming of their own accord. "Yes, Jordan..." She cleared her throat. "I will marry you." She tried the sentence again. "Yes, Jordan... my darling, Jordan. I will marry you."

Elise threw the covers off and sat up in bed, her eyes wide with wonder. Suddenly the words had become easier to say. "Yes, yes, yes. Of course I'll marry you." A smile touched her lips. "I would love to marry you, Jordan Prentiss. I would love to be your bride."

Elise closed her eyes. Could she do it? Could she trust her instincts and Esme's assurances? The prospect of a future without Jordan was inconceivable. She loved him like no other and she could never forget him, no matter how hard she tried.

Yes! She would do it! She would marry Jordan Prentiss, and come hell or high water, they would live happily ever after.

Elise opened her eyes and grabbed the bedside phone. Now she just had to get him to propose once more. She giggled at the thought of his reaction when she finally said yes. Pausing to savor the image, she let her thoughts drift back over the past two months. The wedding plans were all made, each detail carefully considered with her own tastes in mind, right down to the wedding dress. It was as if fate had ordained that she would be his bride all along.

Maybe there was magic at work here, she said to herself.

She quickly dialed Jordan's home phone number as she concocted an excuse for them to meet just once more. The phone rang only once before she hung up, doubt slicing through her.

You're being rash and reckless.

Calming her nerves, she dialed his number again. This time she let the phone ring twice before she hung up. What if she was making a mistake?

Take a chance, Elise. You love him.

She dialed once again. The phone rang four times before she heard a click on the other end of the line. Her heart jumped into her throat. Jordan's voice sounded a stilted greeting and her heart fell back into place with a disappointed *plop* when she realized she had reached his answering machine. As the tone sounded, she opened her mouth, ready to leave a message. But the words refused to leave her lips, and in the end, she hung up.

With a moan of frustration, she got up from the bed and walked to the window, then pushed aside the lace curtains and gazed down at the street. Lazy snow- flakes drifted on the midnight air, falling softly to the street below, dusting the gray concrete in glittering white. Snowfalls used to bring out the romantic in her, making her feel all cozy and safe. But now a smother- ing sense of loneliness swept over her and she shivered and wrapped her robe more tightly around her for pro- tection against the draft of cold air at the window. She bent over the radiator and placed her palm on the barely warm cast iron.

No wonder she was cold. A nice cup of hot tea would set things straight. So would a good night's sleep. Maybe fate had stepped in again. Maybe she wasn't meant to talk to Jordan tonight.

Elise made her way to the dimly lit kitchen and set the tea kettle on the stove to boil water. She slid onto one of the kitchen stools. Minutes later, the heat from a cup of chamomile warmed her face and hands and soothed her warring emotions.

Her mind roamed back to the final scene from the movie and she let her imagination spin a wonderfully romantic scene between Jordan and her. He would appear at her door. She would be stunned at first, then without a word, he would sweep her into his arms, kissing her deeply, enfolding her in his strong embrace. She would be spellbound, unable to speak. Then he would—

Her moony daydreaming was interrupted by the sound of the doorbell. Her heart stopped. Only one person would appear at her door after midnight. Elise walked slowly to the foyer. With a tremor of indecision, She reached for the doorknob, then pulled her hand away. Her fingers shook as she tugged the lacy curtain away from the window beside the door and peeked into the darkness. Her heart hammered in her chest.

A shadowy form stood on her stoop beneath the soft glow of the porch light, sparkling snowflakes falling against a familiar navy cashmere topcoat and dark hair. Slowly she unlocked the dead bolt, released the chain and turned the doorknob. A sweep of snow blew into the foyer as she opened the door.

An uncontrollable shiver ran through her, but it was caused by fear more than the cold, for Elise's future stood waiting on her front steps.

8

ELISE WASN'T SURE how she ended up in his arms or whether Jordan said anything to her before he covered her mouth with his. All thoughts of Ingrid Bergman and righteous indignation fled her mind the instant their eyes met. One moment, they stood on opposite sides of the threshold and the next, she was caught up in his embrace and swept away by his kiss.

Things she knew she should say dissolved in her throat and she realized that the time for talking was past. Talking had only brought them to an impasse, their words like bricks, building a wall between them. Now the wall lay demolished at her feet, breached by his touch and his taste, by the indescribably heady scent of him. It was a dream, a hazy cloud of romance, a fantasy come true.

The kiss went on and on, until the dream was gradually replaced by a very real passion that rose within her. Suddenly, she didn't want the fantasy, the perfect man; that wasn't enough. She wanted a real man, flesh and blood, driven by pure lust and desire. Hard muscle and smooth skin, warm breath and firm touch. She wanted Jordan.

With his mouth still melded to hers, Elise fumbled with Jordan's coat and scarf, until he impatiently yanked them off and threw them down on the foyer floor. He kicked the door shut with his heel and pulled

Elise back against his unyielding body, taking her
breath away as he strained to eliminate all space between them. Parting the front of her robe with one
quick, hungry movement, he skimmed his palms over
her body. His fingers stilled when they came in contact
with the lacy Merry Widow and he stepped back to
look at her. A seductive smile curved his lips and he
quirked his brow in appreciation, before he pulled her
to him again with renewed urgency.

Elise sighed in pleasure, following his lead, running
her hands beneath his suit jacket, over his ribs and
torso, feeling his heat radiating through the crisp,
starched fabric of his shirt. How many times had she
imagined touching him with such delicious abandon,
then chastised herself for such fantasies? But now it
seemed so natural, so right.

Hesitantly she moved her fingers to the front of his
shirt and pushed aside his tie. Slowly she worked at the
row of buttons, her mouth still locked with his. Dragging herself from his kiss, she let her lips follow the trail
of her fingers. With her forehead against his muscled
chest, she inhaled the clean scent of his skin.

When her hands reached his belt, she stopped, then
looked up into his eyes. For a brief moment, she was
surprised at the undisguised vulnerability she saw there.
It was as if she were looking at a different man, stripped
of his icy armor to reveal the human beneath, a man she
had only seen in fleeting moments when his guard was
down. This was the man she wanted. This was the man
she would spend her life with.

Her lips were numb from his kisses, and at first her
mouth refused to work properly, but she felt compelled to speak, to set everything right between them.

What would happen this night would have meaning. This was the beginning of their life together. "Jordan, I—I have something I need to—to tell you."

He placed a finger firmly over her lips. "So help me, Elise, if you're going to grade me on my kissing, you'd better run for cover right now."

She looked at him, wide-eyed, then quickly shook her head.

"Good. Whatever you have to say can wait. Now, close that sweet mouth of yours and kiss me."

Her next words escaped from behind his finger. "Bub iz impordant."

"Elise." His voice held an unmistakable warning and he replaced his finger with his mouth, effectively stopping all further conversation. Without another thought, Elise wrapped her arms around his neck and threw herself into the kiss, reveling in the taste of him. She would tell him later.

He pushed her robe off her shoulders and it slid to the floor about her feet. His hands explored her body, her skin tingling beneath the lace, the garment transmitting the heat from his questing fingers yet barring his touch. As he drew her silk-clad leg up along his, she shivered at the delicious feel of his hard thigh against hers. For the first time in her life, she understood the appeal of lace and silk and sexy lingerie. The fabrics seemed to intensify every touch.

She tugged at his clothes, refusing to interrupt their kiss, until his jacket, tie and shirt lay in a heap on top of his coat. His skin was warm and smooth, his chest finely muscled. Then she moved to unbuckle his belt, hearing his sharp intake of breath as her fingers worked against the taut ridges of his abdomen. The belt slithered out of the loops and she dropped it on the floor.

Their kiss was suddenly broken when he scooped her up into his arms. With a tiny cry of surprise, she clasped her arms around his neck, afraid that he might drop her. But his hold tightened beneath her, strong and sure, and she nuzzled her face against his neck, enthralled by the pure romance of being swept off her feet. After all they had been through, she was amazed at how safe she felt in his arms, how right this all seemed. She belonged with him, now and forever.

He turned his head to the touch of her lips on his jawline. "Where's your bedroom?" he murmured as he moved down the long hallway to the back of the house and the kitchen.

Through the sleepy haze of her passion, Elise lifted her head and looked around. "No. It's upstairs."

He walked back to the stairway and stood at the bottom, turning his wary gaze to her. "Second floor?"

"Third," she said with a smile. "Maybe I should walk."

"Maybe you should go back to what you were doing."

With a low laugh, Elise playfully bit him on the earlobe, then traced the contours of his ear with her tongue. She heard his breath quicken and a moan rumbled in his chest as he reached the first landing. He wanted her as much as she wanted him. The bedroom seemed miles away.

"Are you sure you don't want me to walk?" she whispered into his wet ear. "You sound like you're tiring."

"Sweetheart, I'm anything but tired. Besides, I don't plan to let you out of my arms anytime soon."

Jordan started up the second flight of stairs as Elise continued her tender assault on his neck. When they reached the second-floor landing, he lowered her to the floor. Her heartbeat fluttered with nervous anticipation. "Why are we stopping?" she whispered.

"I need a break."

"Would you like me to carry you the rest of the way?"

He growled and settled Elise on the step above him, then moved between her thighs and pushed her back against the stairs, his arms braced on either side of her head. His voice was deep and husky. "I'm not tired. I'm just not sure I can go on in this condition." He pressed his hips between her legs and she could feel the solid ridge of his arousal as it made contact with her most intimate spot, separated only by the clothing they still wore. She somehow knew they would be doing a lot more than resting if he had his way.

He bent over her, outlining the shape of her mouth with his tongue, biting at her lower lip until she responded in kind, running her tongue along the smooth ridge of his teeth, sampling the flavor of his mouth. When she released him, he drifted down the length of her body and came to rest below her on the stairs.

With nimble fingers, he flipped each garter open, then slowly ran his palms along her legs, gathering the silk stockings in his fists until they bunched at her ankles. Then he drew them off her feet, one by one, and tossed them over his shoulder. A delicious shiver skittered up along her spine as his hands slid from her ankles to the soft skin of her inner thighs, gently kneading. Then his fingers grazed her satin panties and probed against the damp fabric until he found the hidden nub of her passion. Elise swallowed convulsively.

She had imagined this moment with Jordan so many times and each time the fantasy was bathed in a misty, magical haze. But that haze was gone. Instead her senses were sharpened until every touch, every sound shot pure sensation to her core.

"You're so soft, so warm," he murmured, his mouth against her knee, his breath soft against her bare leg. He tugged the black lace panties off.

With his gaze locked on her face, he began a gentle assault, his fingers dipping into and dancing over her pulsing center. His eyes smoldered with tightly leashed desire and she watched her every reaction reflected in his intense expression. She grasped his shoulders as the tension began to build, then pulled him more closely, desperate for more. She felt herself sliding down into a whirlpool of mindless sensation as her hips arched to his touch.

Jordan guided her legs around his shoulders and quickened his movements. When his touch was replaced by his tongue, she cried out his name once, low and urgent, before spasms of pleasure overtook her. Wave after wave of drenching sensation washed through her as she shuddered in release.

For a long time, she remained perfectly still, her eyes closed. Drawing deep gulps of air, she tried to steady her pulse. When she opened her eyes, he was beside her, watching her. He raised his hand to smooth a damp tendril from her temple, brushing his lips over her forehead and pausing a moment to taste the sheen of perspiration that dotted her brow.

When he drew back, she looked into his pale gaze. His eyes were dusky with desire and he smiled crookedly when she reached out to caress his cheek with her fingertips. A sudden, aching need twisted inside her and she caught herself stopping the words that she longed to say. She wanted to tell him how much she loved him, but she knew that her words would bring no response. He couldn't say what she needed to hear. And she would not ask him to lie.

She put her arms around his neck and he picked her up again, completing their trip to her bedroom. He set her down before him, then tugged the Merry Widow down over her hips until it rested on the floor at her ankles. She stepped out of it and heard his slow release of breath as he gazed up at her naked body. A sudden rush of modesty coursed through her.

"You're beautiful," he said as he stood, his voice filled with awe.

His words brought back the memory of the same declaration he'd made when he'd first seen her in the wedding dress. Then she had thrilled at the compliment as a naive girl might. But standing before him, flushed with passion, she felt a woman's pride in his appreciation of her body. He reached out to cup her breasts in his hands, languorously teasing at the nipples with his thumbs.

She ran her fingertips down his chest, feeling the light dusting of dark hair, soft and springy under her fingers, following the trail as it narrowed and disappeared beneath his waistband. How long would it take before she knew every inch of his body? She longed to take her time with him, to explore his skin and the muscles beneath, but the desire that had been so quickly sated was now building in her again.

With a flick of her fingers and a wicked smile, she unhooked his trousers and unzipped them with tantalizing leisure, casually brushing against the hard length hidden behind the fine fabric. She felt his hand clamp around her wrist and pull her away.

His movements were unhurried as he removed the rest of his clothes and she stared at him openly. Lord, he was beautiful. Wide shoulders tapered to a flat abdomen and narrow hips. Her eyes came to rest on the evidence of his arousal, smooth and hard, a shaft of silky steel.

His fingers gripped her shoulders and he pushed her back onto the bed. The heavy weight of his body sank down on top of her. Pulling her legs around his waist, he settled himself between her thighs and plundered her mouth with another exhausting kiss.

"I want you, Elise," he murmured against her swollen lips. "Here, now, so much I can't stand it."

She wriggled her hand between their bodies and wrapped her fingers around his throbbing erection, gently guiding it to her moist entrance.

"We need protection," he whispered.

"No, it's all right," Elise replied in a husky voice. They would be married in less than a month. And Jordan had wanted children. "You've been...careful in the past, haven't you?"

"Yes," he breathed. "Always. You're sure it's all right?"

"I've never been more sure of anything in my life." Her words were true on not just a physical level, but on an emotional plane, too. She was sure that she wanted him, his body, his soul, his mind, his children. All that the future held for them. Whether he chose to admit it or not, she knew there were feelings between them, deep and abiding. Maybe it would take a month or maybe even a year, but he would say the words and he would mean them. And there would be no lies between them, only the precious truth of his long-awaited realization.

In an act of slow, carnal torture, he slipped inside of her, expelling a tightly held sigh. As he began to move, Elise felt her grip on reality loosen and once again she was transported into a potent world of pure sensation. She moved with him, absorbing his every thrust, feeling her world spiral upward until at last his body tensed above hers. He froze, his muscles taut, his eyes squeezed tightly shut.

With a soft plea of need, she urged him on until his control shattered, carrying her higher until they both found their release in a rare and precious moment of exquisite intimacy.

JORDAN OPENED his eyes to the soft light that filtered through the bedroom window, then closed them with a contented sigh. A weight moved across his chest above the blanket and he reached out to pull Elise's arm back beneath the covers. Instead his hand came to rest on a soft mass of fur. He opened his eyes again to find a huge gray cat sitting on his chest, staring at him with curious amber eyes. The cat began to purr and a soft rumble vibrated against his ribs, mixing with the quiet breathing of the woman tucked in the crook of his arm. The other cat paced back and forth across the end of the bed and pounced whenever he moved his toes.

"'Morning," he muttered, watching the cat guardedly and trying to remember the animal's name.

It stood up, walked the length of his chest and came
nose to nose with him. Elise moaned softly in her sleep
and the feline glanced her way before training her gaze
back on Jordan. With an audible sniff of disdain, the
cat flicked her fluffy tail and launched herself off his
chest to land with a soft thud on the floor. Seconds
later, the other cat followed suit, leaping from the bed
and disappearing from the room.

He sank back against the pillows, closed his eyes and
pulled Elise's pliant body closer to his, enjoying the
petal-soft feel of her bare skin against the length of his
body. They had made love through most of the night,
tumbling from the bed to the floor and back to the bed
again, until they were both exhausted.

He had lost himself in the warm depths of her body,
drinking in her sweetness as would a man dying from
thirst. It had never been like this with a woman before,
so pure and intense, an unquenchable need that burned
from deep within him. Their bodies had come together
in one incredible passion after another. Yet it wasn't just
his body that felt fully sated. His heart was content
along with his soul. For the first time in a very long
time, he felt happy.

A nagging thought crossed his mind and Jordan
paused to consider a startling realization. Pushing
himself up to a sitting position, he shook the sleep from
his fuzzy mind. Though he tried to ignore it, the con-
cept refused to leave his waking brain: he still wanted
Elise more than anything in the entire world.

Good God. He was in love her. That was the only
explanation for these feelings of raging desire and utter

contentment. He found it almost impossible to fathom, but now, given the choice, he realized he would choose to stay in this bed forever. He would forgo his business, his former life. As far as he was concerned, Elise was all he needed to live, save food and water. Elise *was* his life.

Jordan rubbed his eyes and shook his head again. But there it was. He loved her. Could it be that simple? He grinned. If he hadn't been so damn determined to entice her into marrying him without a pronouncement of love, maybe he would have seen it sooner.

Jordan turned to Elise and shook her gently. She mumbled and turned away from him, snuggling her backside against his hip.

He poked at her shoulder. "Elise, wake up. Elise!"

"Umm," she moaned, burying her face in her pillow.

"Elise, we have to talk."

"Talk later," she murmured.

"Elise, I love you."

"I love you, too," she replied in a sleepy voice.

He raised his voice to a shout. "Elise, wake up!"

Elise jumped as if startled from a deep dream, then turned over, pushing herself up and staring at him through her tangled hair.

"I love you," he repeated.

She regarded him cautiously, as if she hadn't quite heard him, or had heard his words but didn't believe them. "What did you say?"

Jordan jumped out of bed, grabbed his trousers and yanked them on, then turned to her. A rush of self-doubt coursed through him at her wide-eyed stare and he raked his fingers through his hair excitedly. "It's all so simple. Don't you see? I don't know why I didn't say it before."

"Say what? Jordan, what are you talking about?" All traces of sleep had left her voice. She was alert and watchful.

Hesitation constricted his throat, but he ignored it and plunged ahead. "Elise . . . I—I love you . . . I think. No, I'm sure. I love you."

Hurt shot through her expression at his words and she backed away from him, pulling the sheet up around her naked body. "Don't say that, Jordan. You don't mean it."

Jordan looked at her, stunned by the cold tone of her voice. "Yes, I do."

"No, you don't. You're lying."

"I'm not lying."

"You're so desperate you'd say anything to get me to agree to your proposal. You don't love me."

"Dammit," Jordan shouted. "I'm sick and tired of other people telling me what to do and how to feel. For the first time in my life, I know exactly what I want. Elise, I want you to be my wife. If I say I love you, then I love you."

"You do not!" she shouted, scrambling out of bed and dragging the sheet with her. "How can you lie to me? You told me once that we would always be honest with each other. I thought I could trust you," she continued, her voice cracking with emotion. A tear sprang from the corner of her eye and she brushed it away with the back of her hand. "If there was one thing I could always depend on from you, it was the truth."

She wrapped the sheet around chest and tucked the edge in. The tears flowed freely now, yet she ignored them and laughed, a bitter contrast to her weeping. "To think I was going to accept your proposal. I figured if we didn't have love between us, at least we had honesty. But I guess I was wrong. We don't even have that."

"You were going to accept my proposal?" he asked increduously.

She nodded sullenly.

"And now you won't because you don't believe what I just said?"

She nodded defiantly.

Jordan could barely comprehend what she was telling him. She had steadfastly maintained that she wouldn't marry without love. Now, he was admitting his love for her and she didn't believe a word he said.

"Let me get this straight. I tell you I don't love you, yet I want to marry you, and you say you can only marry for love. Then I tell you I do love you and I still want to marry you. And you turn me down?" Jordan rubbed his eyes and looked at her in confusion.

"You don't mean it. You're just saying the words to get me to agree to marry you."

"What about last night? We made love. It was the most incredible night of my life. Doesn't that mean anything to you?"

"It certainly doesn't mean you love me. I'm sure your former girlfriends will attest to that, or did you flatter them with the same heart-felt declarations the morning after."

"Geez, I can't win, can I? I'm damned if I do love you and I'm damned if I don't. There's nothing I can do to get you to say yes, is there?"

He saw the uncompromising set of her jaw and he knew what was coming next. She walked over to the dresser and picked up a silver-backed hairbrush. Nervously, she twisted it around in her hands, her back to him. Her voice was soft and unsure. "You could postpone the wedding and give us a chance to find out how we really feel, without this deadline looming over our heads."

Jordan paused before he answered. It wasn't as if the idea was completely new to him. The thought of giving up control of BabyLove had crossed his mind more than once over the past several weeks. But each time he had written the notion off as irresponsible and overly emotional. Still, the prospect of a future without Elise seemed much more dismal than the prospect of a future without BabyLove. Jordan felt his resolve waver for a moment, then steeled himself to reply. "No," he said flatly. "You know what this wedding means. I can't risk losing BabyLove."

She spun around and met his stubborn expression with one of her own. "So, admit you were lying," she challenged. "Then maybe I'll reconsider." She paused, then hiccuped once and wiped her nose with a corner of the sheet.

Jordan shot her an incredulous look then threw up his hands in disgust. "The hell if I'm going to play your games anymore like some loveblind knight jumping to your every wish." He strode over to her side of the bed and grabbed her by the elbow, pulling her against his body. "I love you. I know how I feel. You're the one who doesn't seem to have a handle on your feelings. Here it is, Elise, your last chance. Will you marry me?"

"If you think you can bully me into saying yes, think again."

Jordan released her arm and she stumbled back. "I give up. Go ahead and wait for your Prince Charming. Wait forever for your perfect man who says the perfect words at the perfect time."

He walked across the room and grabbed his shoes and socks from the floor, then paused at the doorway for a long moment, his back to her, his white-knuckled hand clutching the edge of the door, his pride at war with his heart.

"You don't want a man," he said, his voice choked with anger. "You want a myth."

With that, he walked out of the room, out of Elise Sinclair's house, and out of her life. For good.

ELISE CLUTCHED the note scrawled on BabyLove letterhead. The tersely worded missive had arrived by messenger an hour ago. She read the words again, trying hard to accept their meaning:

Dear Ms. Sinclair,

You will be happy to learn that I have chosen a bride and she has graciously accepted my proposal of marriage. I have passed along all the pertinent details of your wedding plans and she prefers to complete the rest of the wedding responsibilities on her own, including addressing and mailing the invitations. Consequently, she will have no need of your services.

Though my bride is quite confident that she can handle all the plans on her own, I would prefer that you confirm all arrangements and be present on the day of the wedding to ensure that all runs smoothly.

Enclosed is a check to cover your services, including the bonus I promised.

I wish you continued business success in the future.

Sincerely yours, Jordan B. Prentiss

P.S. I hope you find your prince.

Elise crumpled the letter in her fist and hurled it across the parlor. She watched as Thisbe pounced on it and batted it across the floor until she lost it beneath the sofa.

Well, he certainly worked fast. Just two days before, Jordan Prentiss had professed his devotion for her and made incredibly sweet, passionate love to her. Now he was marrying someone else.

Just what had their night together meant? Was it simply a manipulation on his part, another scheme to secure a bride? She had spent the past forty-eight sleepless, tear-filled hours doubting his actions and words, right along with her own, wondering if he had told the truth, wondering if she should have believed him. Now it was painfully obvious that Jordan hadn't lost any sleep over the entire incident. He hadn't meant a single word.

How could she have been such a fool? She had actually maintained hope that he would come to his senses and postpone the wedding for her. How many times had she picked up the phone to call him? How long had she stood by the window and watched for his car? She had even taken a taxi to his office building and sat in the lobby, hoping to run into him, before her pride got the best of her and she rushed home.

You don't want a man, you want a myth.

His parting words echoed through her mind. What was so wrong with wanting it all? Love, devotion, fidelity, commitment. Didn't every woman deserve that much? A man she could count on through thick and thin. A man who would put his wife before everything else in his life, including his business.

Elise brushed a tear from her cheek. Were her expectations that unrealistic? She knew, deep in her heart, how much BabyLove meant to Jordan. He had invested his life in the company and she was forcing him to chose. If he truly wanted her, he would have to choose; she couldn't give in.

But would it be so bad? Having Jordan on his terms would be better than not having him at all. At least she loved him. She might spend the rest of her life searching for a man that made her feel like Jordan did and never find another. Elise clenched her fists. No! It wouldn't work. She didn't want to spend her days playing devoted wife to a demanding mistress named BabyLove.

She felt a surge of tears clot in her throat, then swallowed them back, placing her hand on her chest. Why did it hurt so much? Her heart felt as if it had been torn in two, a sharp, ever-present ache stealing her breath and leaving her emotionally drained.

She hadn't eaten more than a bite here and there since the jelly beans she'd wolfed down before Jordan had arrived that night. Eating was the last thing on her mind, especially in the morning, when any thought of food seemed to induce nausea.

Would every day without Jordan be greeted with the same empty, sick feeling? It was nearly impossible to

pull herself out of bed in the morning and face the day.
Morning sickness. The naively humorous phrase for
her tired and hungry state shot through her mind before she brushed it aside. Then a startling realization hit
her like a sharp slap in the face. She and Jordan hadn't
bothered to use birth control that night. She had been
so certain they would be married and so sure he wanted
children. Her common sense had been blurred by the
overwhelming desire to feel him inside her, without
barriers, to give him what he truly wanted, a wife and
a family. Now that heedless decision had turned into a
horrible mistake.

Elise frantically ran to retrieve the calendar from the
kitchen, trying to remember dates that had meant
nothing to her until now. She couldn't be. Morning
sickness didn't start until much later in the pregnancy,
did it? It was just nerves.

I won't worry about it until I find out for sure, she
told herself as she fished Jordan's letter out from beneath the sofa. Thisbe sat beside her, waiting to re-
claim her newest toy. Elise looked at the cat's expectant
expression, then placed the wad of paper at Thisbe's
feet. Slowly she reached out and gave the feline a gentle pat on the head. As she pulled her hand away, Thisbe
rubbed against her palm and licked her index finger affectionately.

Elise sat on the floor, astonished by the truce that had
been called. The cats had never approached her before; in fact, they had always maintained a wide berth.
But now, this simple act of affection from Thisbe eased
the aching hollowness in her empty heart.

She would survive. The hurt would gradually fade
and the pain would dull over time. She would throw

herself into her work, making a greater effort to find new clients. With Jordan's generous compensation, she wouldn't have to worry about paying her bills for a long time. Maybe she would take a vacation, get away from the cold, bleak Chicago winter. She could visit her father and Dorthi in Florida. She would try to build a relationship with her stepmother. The prospect of lying in the sun and taking long, solitary walks on the beach brought the first glimmer of hope into her desolate outlook.

She would plan to leave the day after Jordan's wedding. By that time she would be sure she wasn't pregnant. All her worries would be put to rest and she could go on with her life as it had been before.

9

ELISE STOOD in the center of the long aisle of Fourth Presbyterian Church. Huge in scope and English Gothic in design, the church was an oasis of tranquillity, nestled among the skyscrapers and stores that lined the Magnificent Mile. She had never attended a wedding at Fourth Presbyterian but had wandered through the church many times to admire the massive pillars and soaring arches, the dark wood and limestone walls. Elise wondered how many brides had walked up the aisle and how many grooms had waited at the altar since the church had been built decades before.

She glanced down at her watch. In about an hour, the guests would all be seated, their presence filling the church to barely a quarter of its capacity. To compensate for the extra space, Elise had filled the nave with flowers and greenery. The fresh fragrance pervaded the still air.

The quiet was broken by the sound of the organ and Elise looked up to the huge choir loft. The organist, outlined against the glorious stained-glass window that spanned the rear of the church, gave her a brief wave before he began rehearsing some of the music she had chosen for the service. She felt a stab of pain in her heart as she recognized the majestic strains of Purcell's "Trumpet Tune," the music she had selected for the processional.

How would she ever make it through this day? Given the choice, she would have stayed home in bed, eating a quart of ice cream for breakfast and trying madly to forget the significance of April 18. But—as she told herself again and again—she was a professional and it was her duty to make sure the Prentiss wedding came off without a hitch. She could fall apart on her own time. Besides, her masochistic curiosity had gotten the better of her and she wanted to see for herself whom Jordan had finally chosen as a bride.

"What a perfect day for a wedding," a familiar voice cried.

Elise lowered her gaze from the choir loft to see Dona walking slowly up the aisle, taking in the magnificent architecture and Elise's choice of floral decorations. "A sunny spring day with no chance of rain," Dona continued. "Elise, the church looks simply spectacular."

She smiled and nodded to her best friend. "It does, doesn't it? This has got to be the most wonderful wedding I've ever planned."

Dona laughed. "You say that about every wedding you plan."

"This time I'm sure," Elise replied in a soft, wavering voice. This would always remain the most wonderful in her memory, eclipsing those from the past and those yet to come. How could it be anything but perfect—this was supposed to have been her wedding.

"Hey, are you all right?" Dona rushed up to her, grabbing her hand and giving it a squeeze.

Elise brushed a tear from her cheek and forced a smile. Dona knew nothing about her relationship with Jordan, except that Elise had once had a passing infatuation with her wealthy and handsome client. His proposal and her refusal, the night they'd spent together and his declaration of love—all these Elise had kept locked deep inside her. "Of course I'm all right," Elise assured her. "You know I always get emotional at weddings."

"Usually you wait until the service starts before you open the floodgates, though."

"I'm just a little overwhelmed by the church and the flowers and everything."

"So, what do you need me to do?" Dona had assisted her on nearly all her weddings, helping Elise cope with the last-minute details and the minor crises that seemed to appear out of nowhere. Today her help would be the only thing that would keep Elise from losing her composure entirely. Dona would deal with the bride and groom and Elise would keep to the shadows, overseeing the other facets of the wedding.

"I need you to go over the usher's duties with them when they arrive. Then I need you to review the order of the service with the minister. Then, when the bride and groom arrive, brief them. They insisted on no rehearsal, but the service is very straightforward and the minister will guide them through it."

"Got it," Dona replied. "Anything else?"

"Yes. I'll need you to coordinate the processional."

"But you always do that."

"Well, I can't today. I have to . . . work with the photographer. It won't be hard—there's only one attendant. Just be sure the groom is in place with his best man at the front of the church, then run up and give the organist the go-ahead. Come back down and send them down the aisle. And don't forget the flowers."

"Elise, I really think—"

"You can do it, Dona. Now I have to go find a phone and clear up some final details for the reception. Why don't you find the minister?"

Elise rushed down the aisle, not waiting for Dona's reply, then took a left, heading toward the wing of chapels and meeting rooms that adjoined the church. Her hasty escape was thwarted by both the photographer and the florist as she stopped to answer their questions and make recommendations. When she could finally pull herself away, she ducked into the first open door she came to, closing it behind her with a sigh of relief.

As she turned slowly around, her eyes widened at the sight before her. Hanging from a portable coat rack in the middle of the room was the wedding dress, *her* wedding dress. Its wide skirt billowed beneath clear plastic, the tiny pearls and beads reflecting the light. The bridesmaid's dress she had chosen hung next to it, a pale sea-foam green gown with a tightly fitted bodice and gigot sleeves that mirrored the bride's dress.

As if in a trance, she walked across the room to gaze at the gown. It was more beautiful than she remembered. Her fingers gently traced the pattern of seed pearls that decorated the Alençon lace overlay. Taking hold of the wide skirt, she spread it out before her, unconsciously smoothing a tiny wrinkle from the folds of crisp, rustling shantung. With a shudder of emotion, she turned away, trying desperately to keep her tears in check.

She was drawn to two boxes perched on a small table. Opening the first, she found the beaded slippers she had worn that night at the bridal salon. To her surprise, the second box held the exact same veil she had tried on with the dress. A small velvet box revealed a hauntingly familiar string of pearls. Elise slapped the lids back on the boxes, then sat down on a folding chair beside the table.

A sense of unease came over her. What was going on? Hadn't his bride chosen her own accessories? Or had Jordan wanted his bride dressed exactly as Elise had for some perverse sense of revenge? For a long time, she stared at the dress, her mind and body numb. Then, at the sound of a door slamming in the hallway, she glanced at her watch.

Startled by the time that had passed, she stood up and brushed away the effects of her despondent mood. The guests would begin arriving any minute. And the bride, considering she would be dressing here, was woefully behind schedule. Elise decided to make a hasty exit, hoping she would be lucky enough to avoid meeting the woman. Just as she reached the door, it opened and her heart sank to her shoes.

But the figure who slipped into the room was not that of a strange woman, but that of an achingly familiar man. Jordan turned from the door, his face registering surprise at her presence. For a long moment, they did not speak, just looked at each other, gazes locked, expressions blank.

Jordan broke the silence. "You're here."

Elise opened her mouth to reply, but her voice had been taken away along with her breath. Her eyes scanned his body, marveling at the dashing sight he made in his charcoal-gray morning coat and pin-striped trousers. A white wing-collared shirt was a startling contrast to his smooth complexion and dark hair. And the pearl-gray waistcoat outlined the hard muscle of his torso. Her gaze came to rest on a diamond stickpin, twinkling from the center of his paisley ascot.

"Elise?"

She pulled her attention from the hypnotic gleam of the stickpin and back to his handsome face.

"Yes?"

"I didn't expect you to come."

"It's my job," she answered, her voice somehow detaching itself from her body. She felt as if she were watching the scene from a distance, emotionless and remote. She realized this would be the only way she could cope with the feelings that threatened to break free from inside her.

"Elise, we have to talk."

She ignored his words, focusing her gaze over his left shoulder. "Your bride should be here by now. Maybe I should go look for her." Elise started for the door, but the touch of hard fingers grasping her wrist stopped her.

"Please, Jordan," she said in a choked voice. "Don't do this. You're getting married in less than thirty minutes. We have nothing more to say to each other."

"There won't be a wedding. There is no bride."

She snapped her head up and stared at him. "What?"

He reached out for her face and rubbed his knuckles across her cheek, as if he felt an urgent need to touch her. "No bride."

"Why?"

"I think you know why," he murmured. "There's only one woman for me."

She felt a sliver of relief shoot through her at his words, followed by a rush of anger. "But the church, the guests. Why didn't you call this off earlier?"

He shrugged and smiled crookedly. "I took a risk. I thought it best to play the hand out. And I hoped that you would change your mind."

"And the letter. Was that part of the game?"

"At the time it was a calculated bluff."

She was speechless, unable to decide whether to be angry or ecstatic, hurt or touched. Had he really been waiting for her to come back to him, to change her mind and agree to marry him?

"Elise, I need to ask you a favor."

His eyes were soft and pleading and she longed to reach out and brush away the lines of tension that creased his handsome features. She waited for the words, certain that he would say them just once more. *Marry me.* She could feel her answer forming on her lips.

"I want you to tell me the proper etiquette for calling off this wedding."

Her heart lurched in her chest and she tried to keep the disappointment from showing in her face.

Jordan grabbed her hands, pressing them between his palms as he looked into her eyes. "I want to start all over. I want to make things work between us and I'm willing to wait as long I have to for you. These last few weeks without you have been hell. I sat in my office trying to work, but all could think about was you. BabyLove doesn't mean anything to me without you. You're my future, you're my life, not some corporation. I love you, Elise. I think I've loved you from the very moment I met you."

Elise felt her heart constrict in her chest. Oh, how she wanted to believe his words. "You'd give up Baby-Love? For me? Jordan, I can't ask you to do that."

"I have a chance at something special with you, something real. When I think about losing BabyLove, I feel angry. But when I think about losing you, I feel paralyzed, like I can't go on. I can start another company, Elise, but I can never find another you. You're the only thing that matters to me now."

"Oh, Jordan." Tears ran down her cheeks unchecked. She wiped them away and took a ragged breath.

"Come on." He pulled her toward the door. "Let's put an end to this farce."

Elise shook her head, backing away from him, her pulse thrumming in her head. "No. I need some time. I have to think."

Jordan frowned, then nodded his agreement. "All right, but make it a good excuse. I would prefer to salvage at least a little bit of my pride. Of course, we'll let everyone enjoy themselves at the reception. That should help soften the blow. And we can return the wedding gifts."

By now, Elise's heart was pounding so loudly she barely heard his words. Steadying her hands, she tugged him by the arm, dragging him to the door. "Go," she urged in a shaky voice. "Wait for me upstairs. I'll be up in a minute." She pushed him through the doorway, then poked her head out. "Jordan. My assistant Dona is in the vestibule. Would you send her down here? I'd like to consult with her about the best way to do this."

She watched as he strode down the hall, his gait smooth and athletic. Then she softly closed the door and leaned back against it, taking a deep, cleansing breath.

Could she do it? A smile curved the corners of her mouth. Yes! She could and she would.

Elise hurried across the room and pulled the wedding dress from the hanger. Tearing off her clothes, she threw them on the floor until she stood in her underwear. Gingerly, she stepped into the heavy gown and pulled the rich fabric over her hips, then slipped her arms into the sleeves. A timid knock sounded at the door and she heard Dona's voice on the other side.

"Come in," Elise called, her back to the door. She reached back to attempt the tiny row of buttons.

The door opened and she waited for Dona to step in and help her.

"I'm sorry," her friend said. "I was looking for Elise Sinclair."

Elise slowly turned and watched an expression of alarm register on Dona's face.

"Elise," she gasped. "What are you doing? Are you crazy? What if the bride walks in here and sees you in her dress? She'll boot us both out of here." Dona crossed the room and grabbed a cuff. Tugging at it, she attempted to remove the dress from Elise.

But Elise pulled her arm away and smiled. "*I* am the bride."

Dona's voice was nearly a shout. "*What?* Elise, you have gone off the deep end. I knew you had a little crush on this guy, but you've gone way too far. Come on, get out of that dress and I'll take you home. We'll call my mother's psychiatrist, and he'll help you deal with this . . . this obsession."

"No, it's true. I'm going to marry Jordan Prentiss."

"Elise . . ."

"Dona," she shot back in the same patronizing voice. "Have I ever, ever lied to you?"

A confused scowl appeared on her friend's face. "No, I don't think so. But if you're really going to marry this guy, how come I haven't heard anything about it? What about that, huh?"

"That wasn't a lie. I just neglected to tell you the truth. Jordan asked me to marry him and I turned him down. Then we made love and he told me he loved me and I told him to get out."

"And the guy still wants to marry you?"

"He'd better." Elise turned her back to Dona. "Here, button me up. Then I want you to put on that bridesmaid's dress. I think it should fit, though it may be a little big. You're going to be my maid of honor."

"I don't know about this. If you want to make a fool of yourself in front of four hundred people, feel free. But I'm not about to get involved in one of your romantic fantasies gone berserk."

"It's not a fantasy, Dona. I love Jordan Prentiss, and he loves me." As soon as the dress was buttoned she spun around and kissed her best friend on both cheeks. Then she opened the the largest box, pulled the veil from its tissue paper nest and draped it over her arm. She grabbed the shoes and the string of pearls and rushed to the door. "I'll meet you upstairs. Now, hurry."

Elise carefully made her way down the hall to the vestibule, then stood behind a side door and tried to catch Jordan's attention. He stood in profile, his head bent to a young man also dressed in a morning coat and striped trousers. She waited until the ushers had cleared the vestibule of guests, then softly called Jordan's name. He turned to look at her. An expression of relief suffused his face as he walked toward her. "Elise, come on. Everyone's inside. We'd better tell them and get it over with."

She drew a deep breath, then stepped out from behind the door, pulling the long train out behind her. Her fingers tightened on the shoes she held in one hand as she watched for Jordan's reaction.

His initial look of astonishment slowly dissolved, giving way to an irresistible grin.

"Ask me again, Jordan."

He shook his head in disbelief and ran his fingers through his hair. "How do I know you won't turn me down again, Elise?"

"Just ask."

"Elise, will you marry me?"

She straightened to her full height in stocking feet and smiled back at him. "Yes, Jordan, I will marry you."

With a shout of triumph, he pulled her into his arms and swung her around and around, his lips descending on hers.

He hugged her long and hard. She watched over Jordan's shoulder as the same expression of incredulity she had seen on Dona's face crossed the best man's face. Seconds later, her friend appeared in the doorway, dressed in the bridesmaid's gown, and tentatively walked toward them.

Elise breathlessly made the introductions. Dona relaxed visibly when she realized that Elise wasn't crazy and that Jordan actually did plan to marry her. Jordan's executive assistant, Pete Stockton, was introduced as his best man and he gallantly offered Dona his arm, pulling her away from Elise and Jordan and giving them a moment alone.

Elise fastened the veil to her hair, then placed her palm on Jordan's shoulder and handed him the beaded slippers. "Can you help me put these on?"

Jordan bent down on one knee and lifted her skirt, cupping her heel in one hand and sliding the left slipper on. "I seem to remember doing this once before. Only that time, you ran out on me." He looked up at her. "You aren't going to run away again, are you?"

"Not a chance."

"You understand that this wedding isn't legal, there's no marriage license. We'll have to do it all over again in a civil ceremony. You won't change your mind, will you?" She could feel his hand tightening on her ankle as he awaited her response.

Elise reached down and placed her palm on his face, caressing his cheek with her fingertips. The worried look on his face evaporated. "No, Jordan, I won't back out on you."

"We don't have to get married today. We can wait if you want."

"But you could lose your company."

"I could still lose my company. But better to risk losing my company than risk losing you."

Elise looked down at him in amazement. "You'd really give it all up for me?"

"For you and only for you."

"You're not going to lose me, Jordan. I'll be with you always, for better or for worse. Even if you do find yourself out of a job, we'll find some way to work it all out."

He slid the other slipper on her right foot, then stood up.

"I guess I'm ready," she murmured, smiling up at him. She threw herself into his arms and kissed him.

"Ahem. Mr. Prentiss, I presume."

Jordan pulled his mouth from Elise's and turned around, keeping his arm possessively wrapped around her waist. A dapper-looking man in a pin-striped suit and red bow tie stood before them.

"Yes, I'm Jordan Prentiss."

"Mr. Prentiss, my name is Lewis T. Stone of the law firm Schumacher and Stone. We handled your grandfather's personal and business affairs along with his estate."

"I'm aware of that, Mr. Stone."

"I have been entrusted to deliver this to you on your wedding day." The man held out a thin envelope. "It is a wedding present from your late grandfather."

Jordan frowned, then took the envelope from the man's hand and placed it in his breast pocket. "Thank you, Mr. Stone. My bride and I will open it with the rest of the gifts."

"You may want to open it now, Mr. Prentiss."

Jordan looked at the lawyer warily, then pulled the envelope back out of his pocket. He handed it to Elise, keeping his gaze fixed on the lawyer. She tore the flap and unfolded an official-looking letter.

"What is it?" Jordan asked.

She glanced down at the signature. "It's a letter from your grandfather."

"Go ahead. Read it."

Elise held up the letter and began to read aloud:

Dear Jordan,
I suppose you're surprised to hear from me, seeing

as how I'm dead, but an occasion as auspicious as your marriage cannot go by unnoticed. I have no way of knowing how long I've been dead, but suffice it to say, considering your aversion to marital commitment, it's probably been a long time.

BabyLove has always been run by a Prentiss and I intend to see that it remains so. As a wedding present, I wish to present to you a stock option that will allow you to purchase 150,000 shares of the company at $3.00 per share upon the first business day after your wedding.

Elise looked up in bewilderment, her eyes fixed on Jordan. "Did you know about this all along?"

"I'm afraid not, miss," the lawyer answered for him. "Apart from the executor of the estate, Jordan's great-aunt, I was the only person who knew of this."

Elise turned back to Jordan. "What does this mean?"

A smile replaced the look of surprise on Jordan's face as he glanced at Pete Stockton, standing just behind the lawyer. "It means that as soon as we are legally married, we will purchase $450,000 worth of stock in BabyLove."

Elise's mouth dropped open. "That's a lot of money Jordan. Do you think you should spend that much when you might lose your job?"

"We'll borrow the money from the bank."

She drew a sharp breath, grasping the sleeves of his coat with tense fists. "You want to borrow $450,000 from a bank! Good Lord, Jordan. I was worried about telling you about the $2,000 balance on my Marshall Field's charge card. And now you want to borrow nearly a half-million dollars?"

He and Pete were smiling as if they were sharing some private joke. A joke she had no way of understanding. "Don't worry. We'll pay it back the same day—right after we sell the stock. Of course, the stock won't be worth $3.00 a share."

Elise brought her fingers to her temples, trying to massage away a knot of tension that twisted there. "Oh, Jordan. This is not the kind of thing to be telling me on our wedding day."

"Elise, BabyLove stock is worth around $56.00 per share. I'll buy it at $3.00 and sell it at $56.00."

Elise's mind whirled in confusion. He was going to buy stock at $3.00 and sell it at $56.00. That meant he would make a profit. She mentally did the calculations. "That's $840,000!"

He laughed, then kissed her cheek affectionately. "No, Elise, that's $8.4 million. The company can't afford to repurchase the stock at market value, so the board will be forced to back down. And if they vote me out later, we won't have to worry. With that kind of money, I can start another company."

"Ahem." Lewis T. Stone requested their attention again. "I believe you'll want to hear the rest of the letter, Mr. Prentiss."

Elise looked down and continued to read:

"'Upon the birth of my first great-grandchild, you will receive a similar option to buy 150,000 shares. As I'm sure you have already deduced, this will give you controlling interest in BabyLove.

Jordan, you've always been a clever and resourceful young man. Now use some of that cleverness of yours and get me a great-grandchild!

Your grandfather,
Jonathan Bradford Prentiss'"

"So, it will be all yours," Elise murmured.

"That depends upon you," Jordan replied. He turned to the lawyer. "There's no time limit on this option?"

"The option will be available immediately upon your marriage, whether it takes place today or ten years from now."

"Don't you see, Elise? Now that we have the stock option, we don't have to get married today. We can take our time—we can plan the wedding you've always wanted, with your family and your friends. We will wait if you want to. I want you to be absolutely sure about this."

"Do you love me, Jordan?"

"Yes, Elise, I love you." His answer was as firm and certain as her question.

"That's all I need to hear. I want to marry you here, today. We can invite my father and stepmother to the civil ceremony." Besides, from the very start, this *was* meant to be *her* wedding.

"Ladies and gentlemen."

Elise turned to see the organist standing at the base of the stairs to the choir loft.

"The guests are getting restless. Let's get started."

Elise walked with Jordan to the far door, where he would take the side aisle to the front of the church. A sudden thought occurred to her and she felt a brief flash of panic. "Wait. There's just one little thing I have to tell you."

The sound of the first strains of the processional echoed through the church and Jordan grabbed her hand, giving it a squeeze. "It can wait, sweetheart. We've got a whole lifetime together." He stepped to the door leading to the sanctuary.

"No, it can't." Elise tried to calm her frantic feelings, pulling him back beside her. This could change everything. "It has to do with the letter."

"Elise, nothing you have to say is going to keep me from marrying you." He gave her a quick kiss on her forehead. "Nothing. Now, I'll meet you at the altar. Don't be late."

Elise watched Jordan pass through the door, with Pete right behind him. She turned to Dona. "I'm getting married," she said.

"Yes, you are," Dona replied. They rushed into each other's arms, hugging until Elise giggled and pulled away. Reaching up, she brushed the tears off her best friend's cheeks. "Why are you crying? I'm the one who always cries at weddings."

"Oh, I don't know," Dona said. "It's all so romantic. You always believed in happily ever after and now all your dreams are coming true."

"It is like a dream come true, isn't it?"

Dona nodded as she toyed with Elise's veil. Then she carefully fastened the string of pearls around Elise's neck and pulled the blusher veil over Elise's face. With a quivering smile, Elise watched her best friend move to open the wide central doors to the sanctuary. She followed her to the doorway, her heart hammering in her chest as her maid of honor began the long march up the aisle. Her gaze raced along the length of the church, beyond Dona, to the man who waited for her at the steps to the altar. Then she put one foot in front of the other and began to walk toward her future.

From that moment on, the wedding passed in a blur. There was a brief moment of confusion as the minister paused to get their names before beginning the service, but from then on, everything rushed by in a jumble of words and music and excitement.

Then the minister pronounced them husband and wife and she watched from behind her veil as Jordan turned to her. Gently he lifted the netting and pushed it over her head. Taking her face in his hands, he kissed her, softly and sweetly. As he pulled away, he murmured against her lips. "Now and forever, Elise."

She smiled up at him, tears spilling from the corners of her eyes. "Now and forever, Jordan."

Then they both turned and walked to the head of the aisle as husband and wife. They proceeded slowly, smiling and nodding at their guests as they walked.

Elise's gaze was drawn sharply to a pink-clad woman in the first row of pews. She clutched Jordan's sleeve. "Jordan, she's here! The lady in pink. That's her, in the wide-brimmed hat."

Jordan looked down at Elise, then followed the direction of her gaze. "Who, Esme?"

Yes. Who is she?"

"That's my great-aunt Esme. She's a major stockholder at BabyLove and is a member of the board of directors. She's also the Prentiss family matchmaker. She's been trying to marry me off for years. She'll stop at nothing for the chance to dance at a wedding."

Elise stopped and turned to Jordan. "She's your great-aunt? The same great-aunt that served as executor to your grandfather's estate?"

Jordan nodded.

"The same great-aunt that knew about the stock options?"

Jordan nodded again. "Yes, she knew about the—" A sudden realization dawned on his face.

They both turned to Esme. The older woman gave them a jaunty wave, then blew Jordan a kiss and winked at Elise. In that moment, Elise knew exactly what it was that had teased at her memory every time Esme was near. It was in her eyes. Those twinkling pale blue eyes. Eyes the exact color of Jordan's. Why hadn't she made the connection before?

"You don't think she orchestrated the whole—"

Jordan shook his head. "No . . . Well, maybe. She could have initiated the flap about my image. She could have talked Edward into the takeover attempt. And Esme knows me well enough to know I'd do whatever was necessary to maintain control of BabyLove, including getting married. But how could she have known I'd fall in love with you? And that you'd fall in love with me?"

They turned to each other, then back to Esme. Jordan's great-aunt gave them a sheepish shrug.

"She knew," Elise answered with a laugh. "Believe me, she knew."

They continued down the aisle, through the vestibule and out the front doors into the sunshine of a perfect spring day. Pausing on the steps, Elise wondered whether this was the right time and place. It was the perfect place, she decided, and plunged ahead. "Jordan, there is one other thing we need to discuss. I tried to tell you before the ceremony, but you told me to wait."

"All right, Elise. You have my undivided attention for the next seventy years or so. Now what is bothering you?"

Elise took a deep breath. "I have a wedding present for you."

"That's very nice," he replied, kissing her softly on the forehead. "What did you buy us? A toaster? A blender?"

"It's not exactly a traditional wedding present. And I can't give it to you right now, because I don't have it yet." She smiled. "At least, not in the literal sense of the word. You're going to have to wait another nine months or so before I can actually give it to you."

He frowned, a look of confusion etched on his brow.

Elise smiled at him and crinkled her nose. "You're going to get control of BabyLove back a little sooner than you thought. We'll have a vested interest in strained carrots by December."

He stared at her, dumbfounded. "Are—are you sure?"

"The doctor hasn't confirmed it yet, but by my calendar, our timing couldn't have been better. Or worse, depending upon how you feel about this."

"How I feel?" In one quick motion, Jordan scooped her up in his arms and walked down the steps to the street.

"We're going to have a baby," he shouted to any passerby who would listen. Pedestrians stopped and gawked as Jordan spun Elise around. Cabdrivers parked in front of the church honked their horns. A small crowd gathered to watch the groom and bride share a passionate kiss as the guests from the church began to fill the steps behind them. A smattering of applause broke out from several of the bystanders, and soon the crowd that surrounded them began to clap enthusiastically.

Rice rained down on them as they ran to the curb where a horse-drawn carriage waited. Jordan helped Elise inside, then swung in beside her. The carriage pulled into the traffic of Michigan Avenue, amid the squealing tires of cabs and the roar of the city buses. But inside, Jordan and Elise were lost in their own private world.

A world where love *did* conquer all.

**Earth, Wind, Fire, Water
The four elements—but nothing is
more elemental than passion.**

Join us for *Passion's Quest*, four sizzling, action-packed
romances in the tradition of *Romancing the Stone* and
The African Queen. Starting in January 1994, one book each
month is a sexy, romantic adventure focusing on the quest
for passion...set against the essential elements of earth,
wind, fire and water.

On sale in February

To banish the February blahs, there's *Wild Like the Wind* by
Janice Kaiser. When her vengeful ex-husband kidnapped her
beloved daughter Zara, Julia Powell hired Cole Bonner to
rescue her. She was depending on the notorious mercenary's
strength and stealth to free her daughter. What she hadn't
counted on was the devastating effect of this wild and
passionate man on *her*.

The quest continues...

Coming in March—*Aftershock* by Lynn Michaels
And in April—*Undercurrent* by Lisa Harris

*Passion's Quest—four fantastic adventures,
four fantastic love stories*

AVAILABLE NOW: *Body Heat* by Elise Title (#473)

Where do you find hot Texas nights, smooth Texas charm and dangerously sexy cowboys?

$ $ $  $ $ $
$ $ $ $ $ $

EVERYBODY'S TALKIN'
by Barbara Kaye

To catch a thief—Texas style!

Somebody's been taking money from Carolyn Trent's savings account, and bank manager Cody Hendricks is determined to find the culprit. Carolyn's bookkeeper, Lori Porter, is just as anxious to find the thief, but when she and Cody team up, she finds his motives are more than strictly business.

CRYSTAL CREEK reverberates with the exciting rhythm of Texas. Each story features the rugged individuals who live and love in the Lone Star state. And each one ends with the same invitation...

Y'ALL COME BACK...REAL SOON!

Don't miss *EVERYBODY'S TALKIN'* by Barbara Kaye.
Available in February, wherever Harlequin books are sold.

My Valentine

1994

Celebrate the most romantic day of the year with
MY VALENTINE 1994
a collection of original stories, written by
four of Harlequin's most popular authors...

MARGOT DALTON
MURIEL JENSEN
MARISA CARROLL
KAREN YOUNG

*Available in February, wherever
Harlequin Books are sold.*

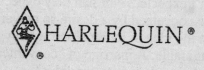 HARLEQUIN ®

VAL94

NEW YORK TIMES Bestselling Author

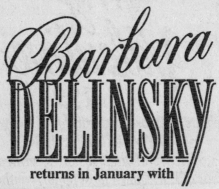

Barbara
DELINSKY

returns in January with

THE REAL THING

Stranded on an island off the coast of Maine,
Deirdre Joyce and Neil Hersey got the
solitude they so desperately craved—
but they also got each other, something they
hadn't expected. Nor had they expected
to be consumed by a desire so powerful
that the idea of living alone again was
unimaginable. A marrige of "convenience"
made sense—or did it?   BOB7

HARLEQUIN®

Relive the romance...
Harlequin and Silhouette
are proud to present

by *Request*™

A program of collections of three complete novels by the most requested authors with the most requested themes. Be sure to look for one volume each month with three complete novels by top name authors.

In January: **WESTERN LOVING**   Susan Fox
                                    JoAnn Ross
                                    Barbara Kaye
Loving a cowboy is easy—taming him isn't!

In February: **LOVER, COME BACK!**   Diana Palmer
                                        Lisa Jackson
                                        Patricia Gardner Evans
It was over so long ago—yet now they're calling, "Lover, Come Back!"

In March: **TEMPERATURE RISING**   JoAnn Ross
                                      Tess Gerritsen
                                      Jacqueline Diamond
Falling in love—just what the doctor ordered!

Available at your favorite retail outlet.

REQ-G3

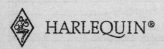 HARLEQUIN®    *Silhouette*

HARLEQUIN®
Temptation

If you missed any Lovers & Legends titles,
here's your chance to order them:

Harlequin Temptation®—Lovers & Legends

#425	THE PERFECT HUSBAND by Kristine Rolofson	$2.99	☐
#433	THE MISSING HEIR by Leandra Logan	$2.99	☐
#437	DR. HUNK by Glenda Sanders	$2.99	☐
#441	THE VIRGIN AND THE UNICORN by Kelly Street	$2.99	☐
#445	WHEN IT'S RIGHT by Gina Wilkins	$2.99	☐
#449	SECOND SIGHT by Lynn Michaels	$2.99	☐
#453	THE PRINCE AND THE SHOWGIRL by JoAnn Ross	$2.99	☐
#457	YOU GO TO MY HEAD by Bobby Hutchinson	$2.99	☐
#461	NIGHT WATCH by Carla Neggers	$2.99	☐
#465	NAUGHTY TALK by Tiffany White	$2.99	☐
#469	I'LL BE SEEING YOU by Kristine Rolofson	$2.99	☐

(limited quantities available on certain titles)

TOTAL AMOUNT	$
POSTAGE & HANDLING	$
($1.00 for one book, 50¢ for each additional)	
APPLICABLE TAXES*	$
TOTAL PAYABLE	$
(check or money order—please do not send cash)	

To order, complete this form and send it, along with a check or money order for the total above, payable to Harlequin Books, to: *In the U.S.*: 3010 Walden Avenue, P.O. Box 9047, Buffalo, NY 14269-9047; *In Canada*: P.O. Box 613, Fort Erie, Ontario, L2A 5X3.

Name: _____

Address: _____ City: _____

State/Prov.: _____ Zip/Postal Code: _____

*New York residents remit applicable sales taxes.
 Canadian residents remit applicable GST and provincial taxes.

LLF

**Fifty red-blooded, white-hot, true-blue hunks
from every State in the Union!**

Look for MEN MADE IN AMERICA! Written by some
of our most poplar authors, these stories feature fifty of
the strongest, sexiest men, each from a different state in
the union!

Two titles available every other month at your favorite
retail outlet.

In January, look for:

DREAM COME TRUE by Ann Major (Florida)
WAY OF THE WILLOW by Linda Shaw (Georgia)

In March, look for:

TANGLED LIES by Anne Stuart (Hawaii)
ROGUE'S VALLEY by Kathleen Creighton (Idaho)

You won't be able to resist MEN MADE IN AMERICA!

HARLEQUIN®

Don't miss these Harlequin favorites by some of our most distinguished authors!
And now, you can receive a discount by ordering two or more titles!

HT#25409	THE NIGHT IN SHINING ARMOR by JoAnn Ross	$2.99	☐
HT#25471	LOVESTORM by JoAnn Ross	$2.99	☐
HP#11463	THE WEDDING by Emma Darcy	$2.89	☐
HP#11592	THE LAST GRAND PASSION by Emma Darcy	$2.99	☐
HR#03188	DOUBLY DELICIOUS by Emma Goldrick	$2.89	☐
HR#03248	SAFE IN MY HEART by Leigh Michaels	$2.89	☐
HS#70464	CHILDREN OF THE HEART by Sally Garrett	$3.25	☐
HS#70524	STRING OF MIRACLES by Sally Garrett	$3.39	☐
HS#70500	THE SILENCE OF MIDNIGHT by Karen Young	$3.39	☐
HI#22178	SCHOOL FOR SPIES by Vickie York	$2.79	☐
HI#22212	DANGEROUS VINTAGE by Laura Pender	$2.89	☐
HI#22219	TORCH JOB by Patricia Rosemoor	$2.89	☐
HAR#16459	MACKENZIE'S BABY by Anne McAllister	$3.39	☐
HAR#16466	A COWBOY FOR CHRISTMAS by Anne McAllister	$3.39	☐
HAR#16462	THE PIRATE AND HIS LADY by Margaret St. George	$3.39	☐
HAR#16477	THE LAST REAL MAN by Rebecca Flanders	$3.39	☐
HH#28704	A CORNER OF HEAVEN by Theresa Michaels	$3.99	☐
HH#28707	LIGHT ON THE MOUNTAIN by Maura Seger	$3.99	☐

Harlequin Promotional Titles

#83247	YESTERDAY COMES TOMORROW by Rebecca Flanders	$4.99	☐
#83257	MY VALENTINE 1993	$4.99	☐
	(short-story collection featuring Anne Stuart, Judith Arnold, Anne McAllister, Linda Randall Wisdom)		

(limited quantities available on certain titles)

	AMOUNT	$
DEDUCT:	10% DISCOUNT FOR 2+ BOOKS	$
ADD:	POSTAGE & HANDLING	$
	($1.00 for one book, 50¢ for each additional)	
	APPLICABLE TAXES*	$ _____
	TOTAL PAYABLE	$ _____
	(check or money order—please do not send cash)	

To order, complete this form and send it, along with a check or money order for the total above, payable to Harlequin Books, to: **In the U.S.:** 3010 Walden Avenue, P.O. Box 9047, Buffalo, NY 14269-9047; **In Canada:** P.O. Box 613, Fort Erie, Ontario, L2A 5X3.

Name: _____

Address: _____ City: _____

State/Prov.: _____ Zip/Postal Code: _____

*New York residents remit applicable sales taxes.
Canadian residents remit applicable GST and provincial taxes.

HBACK-JM